I0626333

THE CHRISTMAS PROMISE

GINI ATHEY

ABOUT THE BOOK

Can a failed promise open hearts and renew a family?

Charlotte Wilson has always lived by the adage, promises made, promises fulfilled. As a successful defense lawyer, she's in great demand and takes on many high-profile cases that send her all over the country. Now, a jury has found a defendant guilty because she missed a critical piece of evidence.

With her world crashing around her—and a video clip of her running from the courthouse to prove it—Charlotte hurries to Willow Birch, Wisconsin, where her husband, a popular novelist, is with his ill mother. Her school-teacher daughter is there, too, with a surprise of her own.

As the holidays approach, Charlotte confronts decisions that will change her marriage and her bond with her daughter and her mother-in-law in big ways. Maybe even for the better.

To families who work hard to keep their promises.

ACKNOWLEDGMENTS

First, and always, to my husband, Gary. He listens to my joys and fears and encourages me to follow my dreams.

Thank you to the many readers who have purchased books and uploaded reviews. As I write, I always think of entertaining you.

I have important close writer friends that I call on when the writing becomes difficult: Kate Bowman, Virginia McCullough, and Barbara Raffin. As the years pass, you become more important to me.

As a member of the Women's Fiction Writers Association and the Romance Writers of America, Wisconsin Chapter, I thank the members for the work they do to support writers both creatively and with the business side of writing.

And shouts of joy to Maria Connor, virtual assistant and production manager, for her guidance and attention to all the pesky details. She always has wonderful ideas.

Gini Athey
2019

NOTE TO READERS

Dear Reader,

Charlotte Wilson has traveled across the country, creating strategies for high-profile, high-stakes legal cases. She's earned her reputation, and she finds the work challenging enough to hold her interest. And maybe she enjoys the flattery when she wins another one. As her confidence grows, she foolishly makes promises to clients, forgetting that when it comes to trials, there are no guarantees.

When Charlotte misses a piece of critical evidence, and a jury convicts her client, she runs to Willow Birch, Wisconsin, her mother-in-law's home, knowing her husband is helping his seamstress mother, Sylvia, through a bout of pneumonia. Charlotte and her novelist husband, Gunner, thought they'd adjusted to the long separations her work demands, but her courtroom defeat brings questions that press her for answers. When Charlotte discovers her very pregnant daughter has moved into Sylvia's house, Charlotte is stunned to realize she and Kim are so distant, her daughter didn't even tell her the news.

Charlotte finds herself relegated to household chores as Kim helps Sylvia meet her sewing project deadlines and Gunner prepares for his book tour. In the process of being with her family, she slowly regains her sense of balance. Willow Birch is a welcoming, generous community. Being there for the holidays helps Charlotte see it through fresh eyes.

I hope you enjoy Charlotte's story of seeing her family and her life in a new light—and maybe even putting her on a new path.

Gini Athey
2019

Promises, Promises
In the brightness of the day
And the darkness of the night
Promises spoken
Promises made

In the brightness of the day
And the darkness of the night
Promises forgotten
Promises fade

In the brightness of the day
And the darkness of the night
Promises remembered
Promises paid

—Unknown

1

I RAN FROM THE COURTHOUSE TO MY CAR AND WASTED NO TIME getting underway. I nosed through the parking lot with media swarming on both sides and yelling for a comment. I'd just lost a case. Not just any case, but a high profile one. Now, the son of a prominent family faced more years in prison than he would have if he'd admitted his guilt outright.

Was he guilty? I believed he was, but it didn't matter. I was defending him.

Had I assured his family I would get him released? Yes. And it was as good as a promise, at least in my eyes. But I failed because of one piece of evidence.

As I drove down the street, I wrapped my free arm around my stomach to quiet the jolt when a long-ago memory came up as bright and vivid as when it had happened thirty-four years ago when I was thirteen years old.

"Charlotte, you promised Mrs. Decker that you would babysit Lucy this afternoon." Mom spun around to face me as she towel dried her hands. *The sweet smell of apple and cinnamon filled the kitchen from the pies on the counter. "In this family, we do not take our promises casually. Especially to go off to the new mall for an afternoon with your friends."*

I made one turn after another until I was on the interstate heading north to Willow Birch, Wisconsin, to be with my husband and tell him what happened. He'd been there for two weeks already because his mother was suffering from pneumonia. I'd planned to return to our home in Minneapolis after a celebratory dinner with my colleagues and a good night's rest, but since I'd failed miserably, I had no reason to stay. I drove on autopilot and only noticed the fuel light on the dash when it began to blink and beep incessantly.

Startled, I realized that while I was going over and over what had happened in the courtroom, I'd traveled north more than two hundred miles, which brought me deep into Wisconsin. The interstate bringing me closer to Willow Birch sometimes skirted the western shore of Lake Michigan, where I saw waves crashing onto the dunes. Pockets of red sumac followed the fence lines along the roadside and stood as signs of the changing seasons. I left the highway at the next exit, knowing I'd be stranded on the shoulder if I didn't refuel right now.

When the pump clicked full, I pulled my receipt and maneuvered into an out-of-the-way space near the building. I needed to gather my thoughts before making two phone calls. Calls that would take more than a few minutes. Realizing I was thirsty, I went inside the store and spotted a bank of coolers along the back wall. I pulled out a bottle of water and opened it and took a long gulp, and let the cold water soothe my parched throat. I grabbed a second bottle and added a bag of trail mix and two packages of peanut butter rounds to my purchase.

Walking back to my car, I rested my back against the driver's door and debated which call to make first. I chose the easy one. No luck. It went to voice mail, so I left a message for my husband, telling him I'd changed my plans and would be in Willow Birch in an hour. I needed to see Gunner now. I had to tell him what had happened in court.

Then I called the law firm in Chicago. I was working with

another lawyer from that office on the case I'd just lost. As an evidence analyst, I'd been hired by the family to oversee the evidence and develop a defense strategy. I kept trying to tell myself that I'd successfully defended a celebrity in California only three days before landing in Chicago for another trial. Even to me, that sounded weak and defensive, even childish. If I was burned out or overbooked, I should have declined the case.

So why hadn't I? If I was truthful, it was part ego and partly my belief about promises made, promises fulfilled, so deeply instilled in me.

After three rings, the receptionist answered. "Davis Three. How may I direct your call?"

In spite of everything, I chuckled. Only Stacy Davis could answer the phone of the Davis, Davis, and Davis firm in the abbreviated form. Stacey's grandfather, father, and brother were the principals of the firm, which employed more than twenty lawyers with myriad support staff. Stacy had told me she wanted to be the fourth Davis painted on the door. Her bright smiles and engaging personality were a welcome change to the otherwise solemn office atmosphere.

"Hi, Stacy. I'd like to speak to Ben if he's around. Tell him Charlotte's calling."

"Oh...Um...They're all in conference, but I'll see if Granddad will take your call." The background music was favorite tunes chosen by the most senior Davis. It reminded me of evenings when I watched my mom and dad dance to songs on the radio. Sometimes Dad would dance with me and my sister Barbara.

Ben's strong voice came on the line and wasted no time with pleasantries. "I think you owe everyone an explanation for missing that critical piece of evidence."

"My mistake." As if he didn't know. I swallowed hard. I wasn't accustomed to admitting failure, and the words hadn't come easily.

"But *you* aren't the one who will ultimately pay for the mistake. Our client will."

In a hoarsening voice, I said, "Yes, I understand, Ben."

"I don't think you do," he bellowed. "The reputation of this firm is based on our successes."

"There's nothing more I can say, Ben. I'm *truly* sorry." I winced at the way I'd stumbled over the words.

Apparently not done pointing out the obvious, he said, "You assured that family, my friends, mind you, that you believed the evidence was not sufficient to convict their son."

"But I..."

"Yes, you did." He disconnected before I could say more.

I stood by the side of my car, and for the first time in months, years, if I was honest, I cried. I was tired, defeated, and not proud of my performance in court. Now, all I could think of was my need to spend time with Gunner. I'd been gone for so long I'd lost all sense of connection to my family.

I absently answered my phone when it buzzed. "Sorry to bother you, Charlotte," Stacy Davis said. "Your husband got your message, but your line has been busy. He called to tell you Sylvia is in the hospital and he's staying with her overnight. He can't use his phone when he's inside the hospital."

"Thanks," I mumbled and disconnected.

It had been so long since Gunner and I had talked about what being away so much had done to our relationship, our marriage, and now the person I was running to for comfort wasn't going to be available. I didn't know what to do next. Finally, I settled on our standby. I sent Gunner a text – Luv U Take care of S.

I returned to the highway and started the last leg of my journey to Willow Birch.

———

THE LAST RAYS OF SUN FILLED THE WESTERN SKY AS I DROVE THE main street of Willow Birch. A small town, my husband's family had built the first home there five generations back. After years of being a newspaper reporter, my husband, Gunner Wilson, had become a nationally known and popular author.

I hadn't been to Sylvia's house for over a year. My work as a contract lawyer had in the last few years stepped up, so I was rarely in my own home, let alone Sylvia's. Now that our daughter was an adult and on her own, I'd taken on more cases, and that meant traveling around the country wherever they took me. How strange that Gunner and I had even passed each other in airports once in a while. He'd be traveling on a book tour, and I was off to my next case. Sometimes we had time to talk for a few minutes, but if we were lucky, we managed a long meal together. He'd talk about the towns he'd be visiting, and I would make general comments about the case I was on.

I pulled into the driveway of Sylvia's house to see lights shining in all the visible windows on both floors. Maybe Gunner had left them on in his rush to get Sylvia to the hospital. The door was locked, so I used my key.

I opened the door. "Hello? Anyone here?"

"Mom?"

I heard my daughter call from upstairs. A complete surprise. "Kim?"

"Be right down."

I took off my leather coat and hung it on the newel post.

"Hi, mom."

I looked up to see Kimberly. She was on the second step from the top of the stairs.

And very pregnant.

"Kim? What? Why am I just learning...I mean...why didn't *you* tell me?" Anger rose up in my chest, making it hard to talk. Not only hadn't she told me she was having a baby, she was far enough along there could be no mistake. Had we drifted so far apart that a pregnancy wasn't worthy of a call? And Gunner? He must know about this.

She hurried down the stairs in a bright fuchsia nightgown and fuzzy slippers. Her long brown, straight hair was gathered into a tail at her neck. "Well, if it matters to you, Mom, I didn't tell Dad either. Until I showed up here."

I stood there. Nothing made sense to me. Not my job, my marriage, or my daughter. Everything seemed out of balance. Funny how that word—balance, or maybe imbalance—so often came to mind when I thought about my life.

"By the way, I saw the clip of you running from the court-house," Kim said. "It's all over the news. But when reporters tried to follow you, they say they lost you somewhere on the highway."

I shrugged. "No mystery. I ran away. I lost a huge case today, and my client and the firm are not happy with me." No sense lying about it.

Kim planted a hand on her hip. "So, why are you here?"

I stared at Kim, tongue-tied, not knowing the answer, the real one. But during the drive up here when I hadn't been in a frenzy over the verdict, I'd thought about promises and what it meant to break them. "Now that I'm here, looking at you, with all the changes in your life, I want to tell you about promises I made, to myself and to my client and his family. I need to talk about why I failed them." I grabbed the post. "It's so important that you understand how hard I work to keep my promises, to my clients, and to myself."

Kim cocked her head. "Have you eaten today?"

I considered her question as if it required great thought. Snacks from the gas station were all I could come up with. "I guess not."

"Well, into the kitchen with you. One sick person in the house is enough." Kim smiled and waved toward the stove. "I made a kettle of chicken soup this morning. I'll heat it up."

I tried to make light of what was going on, but my mind wouldn't focus. I sat at the table and listened to Kim chatter on about the children at the school where she worked, all the while stirring the soup.

The elephants in the room seemed to be on hold, maybe waiting for us to adjust to being together again. It wasn't every day I learned I had a pregnant daughter, and it wasn't every day she saw her mother running from the press at a courthouse. The fact was, I didn't lose many cases.

Kim drank a glass of milk and sat across from me at the table. With each mouthful, I savored the flavor of the hot soup. "This is really good, Kim. I bet you and Dad make a really good duo in the kitchen." I spooned more from the china bowl with the daisy flowers around the rim. Sylvia's kind of china.

Finally, with the bowl half empty, I'd had enough of Kim's meandering talk.

"Where's Matt?" So far, her long-time boyfriend hadn't even been mentioned.

"I don't know." She straightened in the chair and crossed her arms over the fairly large baby bump.

"Does he know about the baby, or have you kept the information from him, too?" My voice carried a sharper edge than I intended, but I had Kim's attention.

"When I told him about the baby, he walked out." She tightened her arms. "He's chosen not to be involved."

"Oh, really? Seems to me he's been involved all along, you might say." I put my spoon down. I was no longer interested in food.

"Mom, listen to me. This is *my* problem, and I'll handle it." She got to her feet and rinsed her glass and added it to the pile of dishes in the sink.

"How?"

"The same way other women do it." She wiped her hands on a towel. "I have a job. I'll find daycare. Matt may not be involved, but we'll work out child support. I won't even have to see him."

I knew it wasn't quite that simple, but I had nothing to add at the moment, so I simply nodded.

"Dad is staying overnight with Gram. We hope she can come home soon."

"I know," I said, my voice still less than warm. "When are you going home?"

"After the baby is born." She rested her hands on the back of the chair she'd been sitting in. "I took a leave of absence, and I sublet my apartment until the end of January."

"January? That seems so far away. And then what will you do? And why are you taking your leave now instead of after the baby is born?"

Her hands went from the chair to her hips. It reminded me of the years when she'd tested us to push the limits of her independence. "*I'm* not on trial here, Mom. Maybe we can talk about this another time. I'm going to bed."

She walked out of the room and didn't look back. Was her lack of affection toward me intentional? I couldn't remember when we'd stopped giving each other hugs, at least when we said goodnight. Maybe it had been more than a couple of years ago, I couldn't remember. I knew I was as responsible as she was, maybe more. She was finishing high school when my travel began to pick up, and when she came home on college breaks, I couldn't guarantee being there. But now, when I needed my family for support, she was distant.

All that was true, but for many years my adrenalin rush came from my cases, preparing trials, waiting for verdicts. I didn't allow being away from my family to interfere with the case or my job. I missed them, but at the same time, I tucked them away so I could focus on the people I was hired to defend. Yes, there were times when I probably should have turned down back to back cases, but I was building a reputation, too.

I sat at the table and called Gunner. Voice mail clicked on, so I disconnected and sent a text message – home with Kim – surprise – hope to see you soon.

I washed the few dishes that had accumulated rather than loading them in the dishwasher. I found the hot soapy water and mindless washing and drying relaxing, a change from keeping my hands in balled fists as I had much of the day. By the time I put the last dish in the cupboard, I was ready to get some much needed sleep. If things had gone as planned, I'd be celebrating with my client's family and associates at the firm. Sitting alone in my mother-in-law's kitchen with my pregnant daughter rushing off to bed was not what I'd imagined.

I looked down at my clothes and saw a wrinkled blouse and skirt. I'd left my shoes by the front door with my suit jacket. I had nothing clean to wear in the morning. I'd left the city in a panic and hadn't gone to the hotel to pack my things and check out. The chance of the media following me from the courthouse to the hotel had been too great a risk.

When I made my way upstairs, I went to the room Gunner and I had always stayed in when we visited. With only his things in the closet and his boots on the floor, I thought of it as his room. Thanks to Kim, a set of sweats and a pair of thick socks were on the bed. I recognized the sweats because I'd given the set to her for a birthday gift. I showered and let the water spill over me for longer than necessary. When I used to visit more often, Sylvia had chastised me for my lengthy showers. Waste of water, she'd say. But without her here to notice, I indulged.

I met Kim in the hallway when I'd finished and put on the cozy sweats.

She rubbed her protruding stomach. "Bathroom runs are part of my nights now." She didn't waste any time stepping in and closing the door.

"Good night, Kim." I murmured as I crossed the hall to Gunner's room.

Easily described as a step back in time, the large corner room overlooked the back yard. The soft glow from the security light on the back of the house made navigating the room easy. I switched on the bedside table lamp. The room had all the signs of Gunner's work style. The bed was covered with file folders and pages heavily edited with a red marker. I wondered how he found room to sleep. The desk was also buried in files and pages on both sides of his laptop. An assortment of shirts and jeans hung over the back and arms of a comfy chair in the corner. Those were signs of the present. But signs of the past were everywhere. School and college memorabilia hung on the walls, including Gunner's diploma from the University of Minnesota, where he'd majored in journalism. The memory of graduation day flashed in my mind. Gunner and I announced our engagement and celebrated the day with Albert and Sylvia, Gunner's parents, and my sister, Barbara. I was thrilled and couldn't wait to move into Gunner's apartment following graduation.

I reached up and touched the frame of his diploma and thought of the path we'd traveled since that day, but all my reminiscing ended when a text from Gunner arrived – S resting. Home tomorrow. Want to see you, LV,G.

I lay on the bed, trying not to disturb the papers. I turned my face to the pillow, hoping to smell Gunner's aftershave, but I detected only the fragrance from the soap I'd used.

2

I WAS STARTLED AWAKE BY A KNOCK ON THE DOOR. "MOM? ARE you going to stay in bed all morning?"

I sat up and caught a stack of pages before they fell off the bed. "What time is it?"

"Close to nine."

"Really?" I hadn't slept past 6:00 for years. Even between cases, I kept my habit of up at 6:00 and in my home office by 7:30. I heard the front doorbell chime.

"Oh, that's the UPS driver with a delivery."

I heard her footsteps as she raced, as best she could, down the stairs. "Delivery of what?" I couldn't imagine what kind of delivery would make Kim so excited. By the time I joined her, she had signed for the eight boxes stacked next to her on the floor.

"Thanks, Russ. Have a nice day." Kim waved to the man in the brown uniform.

"Same to you, Kim."

She closed the door and grabbed two boxes from the top of the pile. She moved through the archway into the living room, now sewing room.

I picked up four boxes and followed her. "You know the UPS guy by name?"

She gave me a pointed look. "Small town, Mom. I know most of the people living here. Gail, the FedEx driver, stops around 4:00 if there is a package for Gram."

I looked at the boxes I held. Sure enough. Each was addressed to Sylvia Wilson. Sylvia was a seamstress and made custom clothes and also did alterations. In more recent years, she'd added making costumes for clients. It was October, so putting two and two together, I concluded many of the orders were for Halloween costumes.

Kim sat at a small desk by the fireplace and carefully opened one box. She recorded the enclosed information in what appeared to be a ledger book and entered the same information on the nearby laptop.

Seeing she was focusing on the entries, I moved away. "I'll get the rest for you."

"Thanks. Coffee's ready if you want some."

The second time I went into the living room, I took a closer look. Sylvia's alteration business had grown into a full-fledged sewing business. Most of the room had been converted into a sewing studio. Three different sewing machines were on tables in a U shape around a large cutting table in the middle. A dress form stood off to the side next to a mannequin. I assumed the dress form was the one Gunner, Kim, and I had given Sylvia a couple of years ago as a birthday gift. The shape of the form changed when the person's measurements were programmed into the computer installed on the back of the form.

The corner of the sewing room where Kim sat was the living area of the house. An old stone fireplace had been built years ago on the outside wall of the room, making it the ideal sitting area. Years ago when wood and ashes became too difficult for Sylvia to manage, she had a propane insert installed. We could see the flames through the glass window on the front. A full-size couch and fabric covered chair were angled side by side in front of the fireplace. The small desk Kim was using stood next to the fireplace.

I looked over Kim's shoulder when I set the boxes beside her. "It's kind of sweet seeing how two generations keep records."

"Gram has her way, but I'm trying to make a database of her clients with all their contact information. Easier to find a phone number or an address than paging through the ledgers. But, you know what? Gram has been working for some of her clients for so long that she doesn't have to look them up."

"That's remarkable." I meant it. Sylvia, approaching seventy, hadn't let age slow her down.

"I'd say so. Gram is the best." Kim opened the next box and repeated the process of recording the project and the client.

"I need coffee." I turned to leave. "Has Dad called?"

"Not yet, but maybe he's waiting for the doctor to come first."

I looked at all the boxes lined up along the wall. "Um... Kim? What if Sylvia isn't well enough to sew?"

"I know how to do most of it, and she can teach me the parts I don't. When Dad called about Gram being sick, I knew I had to come and help her. Isn't that what families do?"

She made it sound so simple, and since I had no quick response, I left her to finish. I needed coffee, lots of it, and maybe a piece of toast. My appetite returned overnight. While I sipped coffee, I scrolled through the latest messages on my phone. I anticipated many and, true to form, wasn't surprised to find both voice mail and email boxes almost full. I scanned those from the media outlets who wanted in on the story— print, radio and TV, and online. My delete key got a workout. These same media were knocking on my voice mail door. I had a policy of not commenting on cases, which added to the public's speculations and wild conclusions.

The call from Ben Davis filled me with dread, but also had me curious. Hadn't he made his position clear during yesterday's call? His message was brief, "Please call, new information available."

I flagged the message so I wouldn't delete it and kept going. The final message got my attention: "Borden Law Firm calling. We need your skills for a new case..." She dutifully repeated the contact info.

I made my decision. *Thanks, but no thank you.*

I set the phone on the table to spread jam on my toast. After my first bite, I was sure it was Sylvia's own jam. Almost immediately, Gunner's call buzzed. "Hey, Gun. How's Sylvia doing?"

"Really good. And you? I saw the TV clips."

"Well, I'm better than yesterday," I said with a sigh. "I can't wait to see you and tell you what happened."

"Me, too. We'll be home in maybe an hour or so. Sylvia wants to visit one of her friends in a room down the hall. And Kim?"

I paused. Why was he asking me? He'd known what was going on with her. But I didn't want to start an argument over the phone, so I said, "Busy in the sewing room." I absently wiped the jam off my finger with a napkin.

"She's going to need to more rest when she's closer to her due date."

"Oh, right," I said with a touch of sarcasm. "She's been doing a pretty good job taking care of herself."

"Hey, cut me some slack. I'm a soon-to-be granddad."

Laughing, I added, "Which makes me a soon-to-be grandma."

"Good to hear you laugh. It's been a long time."

He was right. I couldn't remember when I'd laughed over a little banter. "Tell Sylvia we'll be waiting for her to get home."

By the time I ended the call, Kim had joined me at the

table. "Do you need anything in town?" I asked her. "I need clothes and makeup. I'm a real mess."

Kim drew circles on the table with her finger. "No clothes for me...a waste of money. What I have is good enough for now." She rested her chin in her hand. "The baby will need a few things later."

I swallowed the last of my coffee, lukewarm now. "Good coffee. Thanks for making it. But since you brought up the baby, we need to talk."

"You don't recognize it? It's your favorite brand. Dad brought it with him. He was hoping you might be able to visit before your next case."

So much for talking about the baby. But my heart did a little flutter. Even before Kim was born, Gunner had started making sure I always had a supply of my favorite coffee. "Trust your dad to think of that."

Kim sighed. "He told me when he was on tour, he took a bag of that coffee with him so he could be close to you even when he wasn't."

"That was a long time ago before we sometimes ended up out of town at the same time." I gave her a pointed look. "And before he became famous and everyone catered to him."

Kim narrowed her eyes and looked at me like I was talking about someone else, not her dad. But it was the truth as I saw it. "I'll hurry back from town." I put my cup in the sink. My coat was still on the post where I had left it. I slipped my feet into my heels and checked the pocket for my keys. I mused about Kim's reaction to my observation. Being famous had changed Gunner just as sure as being a really good trial lawyer changed me. I'd be happy to talk about it later if Kim was willing to hear my side of the story. At the moment, though, I needed clothes and odds and ends.

My wrinkled suit and heels made me stand out among the more casually dressed shoppers in the first big-box store I saw, but my court clothes were all I had. Fortunately, it didn't take long to find some jeans and cotton tops that fit, plus some sweaters and sweats. I found shoes that felt like slippers and then a pair of real slippers and added them to the cart. The low-cut boots in my size were a bonus find. On my last trip through the racks, I found a light-weight down jacket that was made to fit tight to the body, and I was proud of mine. It was still trim, largely because I worked out regularly and ate pretty well, even living like a nomad much of the time. I detoured to the cosmetics and got myself some makeup and a toothbrush and all the other things that cluttered up my bathroom counter.

As I waited in line, I couldn't miss the whispering and pointing going on. I might have known that would happen. If Kim had seen me run from the courthouse, so would have many other residents of the town. Since everyone in town knew Sylvia and Gunner and I had been married for a long time, many people recognized us. At least the checkout woman limited her questions as she scanned my pile of clothes. "I heard Sylvia was in the hospital. How's she doing?"

"She's better, thanks." I gave her a bright smile to let her know I appreciated her asking.

By the time I loaded my trunk and pulled my car in behind Gunner's SUV, it was mid-afternoon, and he'd brought Sylvia home. As he helped her from the passenger side of the car, I noted she looked just the same. Her signature white braid hung down the back of her purple coat. But she leaned on Gunner for support.

I approached quickly. "Let me help with your things, Sylvia."

She jerked around as if I'd startled her. "You made quite the name for yourself yesterday," she blurted. "Saw the video a number of times on the television."

"Not intentionally, I assure you," I said, keeping my voice dry. Then I followed Gunner and Sylvia into the house carrying her tote bag full of miscellaneous hospital wares. Kim stood with open arms to greet her grandmother.

"Do you want to sit by the fireplace for a while?" Kim asked, pointing to the sewing room. "Or would you rather rest in your bedroom?"

A few years ago when arthritis attacked her knees and climbing the stairs to her bedroom had become difficult, Sylvia had converted the parlor room, as she called it, into her bedroom to make the main level of the house a complete living area. I doubted she'd been upstairs in a long time.

"The fireplace, dear. It was cold in Gunner's car. Must not have a heater."

I caught Sylvia giving Kim an exaggerated wink.

"Nothing lacking in my car, Mom," Gunner kidded. "You were ready to leave the hospital before I had it warmed up for you."

Sylvia stopped at the desk and picked up the ledger to bring it with her to the couch. "New orders, Kim?"

Kim nodded. "We'll be busy, that's for sure. We even got two orders that will be Christmas gifts."

Sylvia eased herself onto the couch and stretched out full-length. Kim pulled a soft blanket over her. "You need your rest. Don't worry about the orders, Gram. I'm here to help you." She tucked the blanket around Sylvia's shoulders. "I'll fix you something to eat soon."

When I saw that Gunner had gone back outside, I followed him. I had all my packages to take upstairs and tags to remove, but I waited for Gunner to get the rest of Sylvia's things from his car. He held a basket of fruit in one arm and a vase of flowers in the other. "Sylvia looks better than I thought she would. How is she really?" I asked.

His eyes drilled me. "You saw her. She's weak and will need to rest a lot to recover."

I took in his sharp words. Gunner had a special relationship with his mother, and I suspected that lack of sleep didn't help his mood.

"I'm going back to Chicago tomorrow. Ben Davis called and said there's new information on the case he wants me to see."

Gunner lifted an eyebrow. "Now? I'm on deadline to get my next book done before the tour for the new one starts next month. Sylvia needs more help, and Kim can't take on more responsibility right now." He'd emphasized each point by counting on his fingers. "Can't you postpone your meeting to help around here?"

"I'll be back," I shot back. "You and Kim are good cooks, and I have zero sewing skills. Besides, all of my clothes and things are still in my hotel room. I need to pack up and check out. I'd have to go back anyway."

"Make a call. Have them boxed and shipped here. That's not so hard."

His words bit, but I could excuse them due to his tiredness and the stress of needing to write his book. Gunner went into the house without offering to return and help with my packages. It seemed I'd chosen the wrong time to talk about my plans, but the lure of Ben Davis's call was strong. I lived to win court cases, and if there was any way to change the final outcome of this case, I was obligated to be part of it. I easily saw myself on a morning TV show telling my side of the story and how we were able to change the outcome. It would add to my growing list of successes.

It took two trips to get my bags upstairs. I took a deep breath to calm my resentment over Gunner's words and then got busy removing tags and hanging the clothes in the closet and filling an empty dresser drawer. I changed into jeans and a soft sweater.

I noticed movement by the open door. Kim stood there. "Gram's resting in her room, and I think Dad fell asleep on the couch. I'm going to rest for a while, too."

"Anything I can do to help?"

"No, but thanks. I'll get the phone if it rings." She stepped across the hallway and shut the door to her room.

After gathering the throwaway bags, I met Gunner at the bottom of the steps. "Kim said you were resting."

"Power nap. Have to get writing. I'll see you later."

"I want to tell you what happened in court yesterday, so you don't think…"

"Later." He waved me away. "We can talk later. I need to work now." He moved up the stairs a few steps, then twisted around to face me. "Mom needs to rest, so do whatever you want to do in the kitchen."

When had Gunner morphed from being a caring husband into someone so harsh—even arrogant? The bigger question was, how had I missed his new attitude?

I sat on the steps and let a few tears escape. Gunner and I hadn't touched each other. No hug. No kiss. No outstretched arm drawing me close and showing me he was happy to see me. My daughter hadn't given me a warm welcome, either. Why?

Even Sylvia had been distant. I loved Sylvia, but being near her had made me feel small. Always, for as long as I'd known her. Not physically small, we were about the same size, but Sylvia could do everything…really well. She'd had boundless energy and made the most of her days. I felt outside that three-generation trio of family that would soon be four generations. Shouldn't I be more excited about becoming a grandmother? I didn't feel the tingly excitement I had heard some women talk about when they'd heard the news they'd soon be a grandma.

My grandparents had passed on before I was old enough to remember them. Gunner and I had a gallery of pictures on the wall in our condo in Minneapolis, but that didn't tell us what kind of people they were. I wished I knew more now. Mom tried to tell us about her mom and grandma, but

Barbara and I were more interested in our world than what seemed like ancient history.

A large white truck stopped on the road in front of the house, so I opened the door before the doorbell was pushed. Large red and blue letters on the side of the truck alerted me that another delivery was coming. The driver carried four boxes.

"Hello," she said. "I have one more box. You family?"

"Yes, Charlotte, Gunner's wife."

"Lucky lady. I've read every one of his books, some more than once." She took long steps back to the truck and returned with the last box. "Looks like Sylvia will be busy. Lucky Kim's here to help." She gave a small wave and left.

I closed the door. Why would a delivery person know so much about our family? Was the woman a friend of Kim's? Kim had made friends with the children of families in town when she spent her summers visiting Sylvia. I should have asked the driver her name, but Kim would likely tell me.

Early on in my law career, I'd learned one simple rule: Ask the name of any person remotely connected or potentially connected to a client's case. Following that rule had served me well. I couldn't remember how many times an incidental name had become important as a case developed. Now I needed to apply it at home.

I quietly set the boxes near the desk in the sewing room and glanced at Sylvia to make sure she was comfortable.

"Thought you'd be gone by now." Sylvia's raspy voice startled me.

"Kim told me you were resting in your room." I avoided a direct answer to her implied question.

Sylvia smiled. "I can rest when I'm dead."

That simple statement had become a favorite of hers over the years. I remember the first time she'd said it and how I wanted to argue the point. The older she got, the more serious she became when people hovered over her and talked about her health issues. Sylvia was a realist, and I admired her for that. She knew she would die someday. That was simply the nature of life.

I thought that at the age of forty-seven, I had a lot of years ahead of me, but I wasn't foolish enough to believe my life couldn't be gone in the tick of a clock. I will never forget the day the police came to my parents' house with the news of the accident that took their lives. I flinched when I thought about not being alive to see Kim's baby—my grandchild.

Sylvia's quiet cough got my attention. "I made Gunner promise me that he would go on his book signing tour. I know enough people that will check on us while he's gone."

"Well, I..." I stopped. Gunner's book tour was the first two weeks of November. I couldn't say where I was going to be then.

"That's all right, Charlotte. Kim and I make a good team."

Right then, I'd never felt so alone. I wanted to be part of that team.

But I wasn't.

How sad. I didn't believe I was a member of the team called "family."

"You two having a good talk?" Kim entered the room with renewed energy. "Wow, Gram. Five more orders. I hope they aren't all for Halloween." She carefully cut the tape on the first box. "Candy, Gram. This person sent us each a candy bar."

"Must be from George Pearson. He called the other day to see if I was still sewing."

"George Pearson? The Judge?" I asked. How small the world could be, but I wasn't ready to say how close.

Sylvia sat up. "George is a good friend. I've made him a Halloween cummerbund and bowtie for his tux going on six, maybe seven years now."

Kim laughed. "Only George would wear something like that and not be laughed at."

My head swiveled toward Kim. "You know George, too? I... I mean the judge?"

"I played with his granddaughter, Lori, years ago when her family came for the summer. How sad she died in that car accident."

"I didn't know." I shrugged. "I just know he isn't lenient on people who harm children."

Kim had gone back to recording the latest deliveries into the ledger and the laptop. "Mrs. Hartford's box arrived, Gram. I think she sent twice the amount of fabric she needs."

Sylvia coughed again. "She wants a matching outfit for her daughter. Theirs isn't needed until January, so we'll put the box in the cupboard." Her hand moved to indicate the double door cabinet in the corner. "Out of sight for now. Tomorrow, Kim, we'll start laying out the first order. Maybe you could iron the fabric tonight."

Gunner called from the kitchen, "Supper's ready. Come and get it."

Already? Where had the day gone?

Kim helped Sylvia off the couch and through the doorway into the kitchen. Gunner put the kettle of soup on the trivet closest to his end of the table. I stood back, not knowing who sat where until Sylvia was seated and Kim sat opposite her. Gunner nodded for me to sit.

The soup was delicious. I assumed it was the same as Kim had served the night before, but this tasted better, richer. I passed crackers to Sylvia and waited for Kim to cut slices from the warm loaf on the board.

Unfortunately, our conversation dwindled to comments about the food, and the three of them debated what to have for supper for the next three days. I limited my contribution to the meal before me. "Kim told me you taught her how to make this, Sylvia. It's delicious."

"I can show you some day. Are you here for the holidays?

Gunner hasn't mentioned it." She looked toward her son, then back to me.

"I'm returning to Chicago tomorrow. There are a few things I need to take care of at the firm, and I still have all my things at the hotel. I was planning to go to Minneapolis after the trial, but with Kim and Gunner here, I came to Willow Birch."

"Why didn't you tell me, Mom? Dad and I would have made a bigger meal for tonight."

"How is that going to change the result of the trial?" Gunner had his spoon ready to dip another mouthful. "According to the newscast, it's over. A done deal, as the prosecutor said."

"Ben told me new information has come forward," I said, defensively. "I don't know what he specifically means by that, but I promised the family that the evidence was circumstantial, and it wasn't enough to convict their son."

"I can't imagine what that family is feeling now." Sylvia lifted her English china tea cup. "To have a son convicted of robbing a store."

"He said he wasn't at the store. But he was. He…"

"Enough, Charlotte." Gunner interrupted me. "We don't need to rehash your case."

"I want Sylvia, Kim, and you to know why I ran from the courthouse. It's not something I usually do."

"Another time, Charlotte. It's time for Mom to get to rest. She's had a few sleepless nights with the pneumonia and the hospital." Gunner finished his water and began clearing the table.

"Me, too, Mom. Gram and I have a busy day tomorrow. I want to be rested. See you in the morning before you leave." Kim helped Sylvia from the table.

"I'm leaving very early."

"Then travel safely." Kim turned back to Sylvia. They were arm in arm, about to leave the room.

"Kim, I need you to understand my—" I spoke to an empty doorway.

"Sylvia and Kim have different needs than yours right now." Gunner held a stack of bowls.

I reached out to take the soup dishes. "Leave the dishes and go write. At least I can do that." I wanted to be alone.

He set the bowls on the table and took a cookie with him when he left. Of course, they were homemade. Nothing store bought in Sylvia's house, and she always had the jar full of her classic chocolate chip recipe. After my first round of transferring the used dishes to the sink, I sat down—in Sylvia's chair —and grabbed a cookie from the plate. After loading the already half-full dishwasher and wiping off the table, I finished the job by washing the kettle. I gave the counter a quick wipe and turned on the dishwasher. I was done.

Not ready to interrupt Gunner's writing time, I returned to the living/sewing room. When Sylvia expanded her sewing from doing alterations to custom sewing, I'd judged her work as amateurish, certainly not the caliber of the tailor I used in Minneapolis. I never told her my opinion, but later, after I had made my initial judgement, I'd seen the clothes Sylvia had made for her clients. One jacket and skirt, in particular, I wanted for myself. Sylvia refused. She said that each outfit was a one-of-a-kind for the client. I argued using all my lawyerly tactics. "What if I promise to only wear it when I'm in Minnesota?" was my last attempt.

Sylvia stood her ground. "It won't happen, Charlotte. I would never break the trust my clients have in me. Not even for you."

I don't remember my reply, but after that, Sylvia made clothes for *her* clients, and I had a few special occasion outfits made closer to home. Now, seeing the dress and jacket on the dress form forced me to admit that Sylvia's sewing was as good, if not better than any tailor I used.

With nothing more to keep me downstairs, I turned off the

lights and headed upstairs. A small light on the table in the hallway provided enough light to move about freely. But Gunner wasn't in the bedroom when I opened the door. His laptop was gone, too. I knew he wasn't downstairs, so he had to have moved to one of the other rooms on the second level. Sure enough. A swath of light reflected on the hardwood floor from under the door of the room in the corner, the one directly above Sylvia's bedroom. Gunner had made it clear that he wanted time to write, and I understood his need for solitude.

I was in my second year of law school when Kim was born. Gunner would take her to the library or the park to give me blocks of time to study uninterrupted. I'd reminded him many times that my degree and career were a family accomplishment. Gunner had struggled to balance his freelance writing with what Kim needed, and it wasn't until Kim was older that Gunner's first book was published. His flexibility in being able to write anywhere allowed me to graduate. Fifteen years later, when Kim was in high school, and after working for a large, progressive law firm in Minneapolis, I began traveling to different states as an independent defense consultant. I raised my hand to knock on the door. My desire to tell Gunner about the court case and my departure in the morning was important to me. My successes had become my identity, and this failure, the first in a very long time, had stripped my self-esteem. Of course, Gunner's writing was equally important to him. I lowered my arm and returned to our bedroom to find that Gunner had removed all the papers from the bed. I checked my phone one last time before shutting off the light. I gave the pillow a good punch and found a favorite position to sleep.

3

SOMETIME DURING THE NIGHT, I WAS AWAKENED BY GUNNER'S voice. "Ouch." He mumbled a few choice words, and a few minutes later, the mattress moved under his weight. He rested his strong arm on my hip. His breathing became steady and smooth as we shifted into our favorite sleeping positions.

I lay awake. Why hadn't I responded to his touch? Had we grown so far apart that even the simple physical acts of love—hugs, kisses, touches—were no longer part of our lives? I didn't move the rest of the night. It was important to me that I not break my connection to Gunner.

I startled when my phone buzzed as a wakeup call. Gunner rolled away and pulled the quilted comforter over his shoulders. I quietly slipped from the bed and grabbed my bag and purse. I would use the bathroom downstairs to dress. At the bottom of the stairs, I saw a light on in the sewing room. I was sure I had turned every light off before going upstairs the night before.

"Hello?" I called out to let the person know I was there.

"I'm on the couch, Charlotte. Couldn't sleep." Sylvia's voice was stronger than the previous day. I rounded the corner of the couch and saw her wearing a flannel robe with satin lapels and lace trimmed sleeves. Her toes peeked out from under the robe's hem.

"It seems you're feeling better today. I wanted to get an early start. I hope to be back by this evening. I'll call if my plans change." I was rambling, but Sylvia's lack of expression had me acting like a young girl home after curfew.

"We can talk when you get back to Willow Birch." She closed her eyes and leaned her head against the pillow.

Talk about being dismissed. Sylvia was better at that than many judges I'd worked with. I didn't argue. I wanted to talk to Gunner and Kim first, but each seemed preoccupied with what needed attention in their own lives.

I finished in the bathroom, dressed in slacks with a matching plaid jacket and my new boots. I made sure the front door was latched before I stepped off the porch. I stopped for a traveling coffee at the plaza next to the entrance to the interstate going south to Chicago and sent a good morning text to Kim and another to Gunner, adding that I hoped the writing went well. I didn't plan to check my phone until I was closer to Chicago. I adjusted my sunglasses and drove down the ramp to merge into the morning traffic.

Halfway through the drive, I'd called to confirm that Ben Davis would be in the office waiting for me. "Yes, Charlotte. Granddad and others have cleared their schedule for the conference with you." Stacy's happy voice took some of my tension away.

As I neared the downtown street where the Davis law firm was located, I became mired in bumper-to-bumper traffic. The sun reflected off the buildings of the city, making them look like shards of gold rising into the sky. Small flutters in my stomach, a recent sensation, gathered speed the closer I got to my destination. I parked in one of the firm's spaces in the nearby lot and hurried to the office.

When the elevator dinged for the fifth floor, I stood aside to let others step out first. If the media were in wait, I was going to return to the lobby and escape. I saw no one when I stepped out.

Thank you, Universe.

I pushed open the heavy glass door into the reception area, where Stacy greeted me with a huge smile. "Good to see you, Charlotte. Everyone's in the conference room, so go right in. I'll ring granddad."

I walked the length of the offices to the large room reserved for meetings. About the time I was going to knock on the closed door, it was opened by someone from the inside. "Charlotte, please come in and take a seat." Douglas Davis motioned to an empty chair next to his. The room was warm, so I removed my coat but kept my suit jacket on. Ben Davis sat at the head of the table. This was not a casual meeting.

Douglas, tall and thin, never appeared stressed or hurried. His up-to-the minute stylish and well-cut suits and shirts fit perfectly. I'd never even seen him without his suit coat on. I wondered at times, and again today, if that was his way to be different from Ben, his father and the most senior Davis.

Across the table from me sat Brandon Murphy, the young lawyer from the firm who hadn't noted the critical piece of evidence. I nodded. After the state prosecutor had used the evidence to support his case and won the conviction, I was surprised to see him. Not many firms retained lawyers that make crucial mistakes.

"Hello, Charlotte. Thanks for coming in today." Ben's voice was strong, smooth, not harsh as I had expected.

I nodded again. I thought it best to remain silent until I heard more.

"We're all busy people, so let's get started." Ben continued and tapped his pen on the table. "Brandon, you asked to go first."

I looked across the table. His hands trembled, but his voice was strong. "Yes, thank you. I'm here to apologize to each of you for my mistake. I take full responsibility for missing the license plate on the car through the window of the store. It was clear and not obstructed in the security picture. I was so focused on the blurred image of the robber that I didn't look closely at the periphery of the picture." He stopped to take a drink. "I'm not going to ask for any special consideration and ..." He pushed an envelope toward the middle of the table. "I have written a letter of resignation if that will best serve the firm."

He looked across the table at me. I hadn't been perfect as a young lawyer. I'd made mistakes, some serious. That was how we learned not to make them again.

"Charlotte, would you like to say a few words?" Ben asked.

I curled my hands into fists in my lap. I was afraid to make another mistake with this firm. "Not at this time." I used the standard no comment answer.

"Douglas? Phillip? Would either of you like to add to the conversation?" Ben directed his question to his son and grandson.

"Yes, I would." Douglas sat up straighter in his chair. "Lawyers work to protect people, and no individual is perfect. Myself included. We all make mistakes. Some mistakes don't cause harm to anyone, and we can learn from them. Then there are mistakes on the other end of the spectrum. Someone loses, and most often those mistakes change a person's life." He stopped to take a breath. "We must be willing to learn from these cases, too. I believe Brandon did not intentionally miss this evidence. We expected him to review evidence that should have been overseen by a more experienced lawyer."

He turned and looked directly at me. I rolled my pen between my fingers then put it down. I didn't need to expose my anxiety.

"Charlotte? Would you like to comment now?" Ben was back in control of the meeting.

I cleared my throat, taking time to organize my thoughts. "In retrospect, I made more than one error that altered the outcome of this case. I made what was, in essence, a promise to the family that should never have been made." Saying that aloud made it all the more real. "That was arrogant of me, and I know better than to assure anyone about the outcome of a case. I saw the same security picture that Brandon worked on. I looked at the assailant, not the surroundings, and saw a fuzzy image that could be any number of individuals. My experience led me to believe that no jury could convict our client on that evidence."

I stopped before I continued with excuses of fatigue and limited time for preparation. "As I've told Ben, the responsibility is mine. I am truly sorry. If I could change the outcome..." I had no more words.

I saw the end of the meeting approaching, but Ben hadn't told us the new information that had brought me to Chicago. I raised my finger to get Ben's attention. He signaled with a nod that I could continue.

"Ben, we've rehashed this case and the responsibilities of lawyers, but so far, you haven't told us the new information you said is available. Or was that a lure to get me here for other reasons?"

The men at the table sat back in their chairs. No one looked at me. I didn't flinch. I wanted to finish this meeting and leave with my reputation as untarnished as possible.

"I have no ulterior motive, Charlotte. The news is that our client's best friend committed the robbery, and it's taken this long and a full trial before he confessed." Ben tapped his pen on the table. "Our client would have gone to jail rather than name his friend. He took your words as a promise to his family, so he assumed neither of them would go to jail. Our client never entered the store. He was in his car the whole time."

I flopped back in my chair. Stunned. I had been wrong from the beginning. I thought of a million questions I'd like to ask the young men, both of them. My emotions began to surge, and before I made more mistakes with this case, I took a couple of deep breaths. No one else seemed surprised with the news, leading me to believe they'd been told before the meeting. "Well, that changes everything," I said as a way of beginning to formulate a strategy for the hearing to overturn the verdict.

Ben kept tapping, faster now. "Brandon will be lead counsel for the court hearing. Your services are no longer needed. Your fee has been transferred to your account."

He'd been polite, but there was no doubt I'd been dismissed. I gathered my things, walked to the head of the table, and when Ben stood, I shook his hand and said, "We've all learned from this case." Everyone in the room knew I would never get a call from the Davis firm again. No one was at the reception desk when I walked out. That hurt. I thought Stacy and I had developed a degree of camaraderie.

I stopped at the hotel. I'd asked that my room be left alone, and they'd honored my request. My room was exactly how I left it the day before yesterday. I threw my clothes into the suitcase and used the laundry bag for shoes and other things. I didn't waste any time checking out.

I recognized parts of the highway as I traveled north back to Willow Birch. My original plan to return to Minneapolis changed when Gunner went to Sylvia's. Had it only been two days ago that I'd run from Chicago and traveled this same route?

I took a deep breath when I pulled into Sylvia's driveway. When I opened the front door, I heard laughter from the sewing room. I rolled my suitcase to the bottom of the stairs and followed my urge to join them. Sylvia and Kim were adding the tail to a black cat costume on the dress form.

"Meow." Kim did a pretty fair imitation of a cat.

Before I let them know I was in the room, Sylvia echoed Kim with a cat cry of her own. They broke into fits of laughter again.

"Can I join you?"

They spun around as if they'd been caught with their hands in the candy jar.

"Didn't mean to surprise you." I pointed to the costume. "Cute cat."

Sylvia looked at me then back to the costume. "You're about the same size as this. Do you want to try it on?"

I hesitated.

"Go ahead, Mom. We need to see if there is enough gusset room for the woman to move around and sit down. I used to try lots of the clothes Gram made, but not now." She lifted her arms and began to remove the costume from the dress form.

The black pants were tight around the hips, but the top fit as if it had been made for me. When I looked in the mirror, all I needed were whiskers and a face mask with the big ears. I made a cat cry and saw Sylvia and Kim laugh in the mirror's reflection.

"What's going on in here?" Gunner stood in the doorway.

I turned to him and gave him another "Meow."

"Try sitting down, Mom." Kim was back in work mode.

The move proved difficult, but we decided I needed more hip room than the client. Sylvia turned away. "We'll leave this on the dress form and give her a call. Maybe she'll have time to stop for a fitting." Sylvia was folding the leftover fabric and cleared off the cutting table. "Time's wasting Kim. See who's next."

"Sit for a minute, Gram. I need a glass of water." She turned to me. "You want one, too?"

Gunner had left the room as quietly as a shadow. I nodded yes. Sylvia sat in her favorite spot on the couch and absently fingered the sewing pins she'd put on her knit shirt. For many years I'd reminded her that the pins were a hazard, but she'd always waved me off. "No time to find the box they belong in when I'm going to be using them again."

Kim returned with three glasses of water. "Well, mom, when are you leaving again? Will it be soon?"

I took a glass from the trio she held. "I...I don't know." I looked around the room, wondering what I'd do if I stayed. My sewing skills were minimal, as were my talents in the kitchen. Yes, when Kim was young, I used a box mix to make her favorite mac 'n cheese and sewed buttons and hems when needed, but that was years ago. Once Kim left for college, takeout and delivery had become our mainstays along with special dinners Gunner cooked on occasion.

"We could use your help, Charlotte," Sylvia said. "I promised all of these people that I would be able to sew for them. I fulfill my promises. Kim can attest to that. But we're constantly interrupted with phone calls from clients that want updates. You could handle that for us. And you've met Russ and Gail."

I couldn't place the names. "Who?"

Kim sat next to her grandmother. "The UPS and FedEx drivers."

"Oh, yes, you're right."

"We need...what do they call them, Kim...those people who keep a business organized?"

"Office assistant? You want me to be an office manager?" I barged in. I couldn't believe Sylvia would ask that of me, a successful lawyer who traveled across the country as a consultant on high-profile cases. Besides, I knew nothing about her sewing business.

"You qualify." Gunner had returned with a cup of coffee and stood in the doorway. "And that lets Kim and Mom focus on the sewing." He took a swallow from the cup. "Anyway, you need to be here when I'm gone next month."

My head felt like it was on a swivel. These people were planning my life, and I had no say? I raised my hand to call a stop to this. "Just a minute here...let me absorb what you're saying." Their idea was moving faster than I wanted. It wasn't my think-it-through, consider every angle style, decision making.

"Are you so busy you can't take time to help your daughter now?" Gunner didn't back down.

"She hasn't asked, but..."

Kim tried to calm the tension that was building. "I'll be fine, Mom. Gram is getting better, and the baby isn't due until December."

"That's not what I'm saying, Kim. My obligation to the case in Chicago is done, and I have another case pending, but I haven't signed a contract yet."

"Then don't. We don't need the money. Why don't you think of what's needed here for once?" Gunner's sharp words hung in the air when he left the room.

"My family is..." I turned to see Kim take Sylvia's hand and stopped midsentence.

An office manager for my mother-in-law's cottage business?

After all my years of building my national reputation as a winning trial lawyer, could I—would I—be satisfied living in Willow Birch helping Sylvia and Kim? A little voice reminded me that it was only for three months. I could use a break from the intense way I'd been living for the last five or so years. Maybe this was a hidden opportunity. I couldn't argue with Gunner about the money. Between the two of us, we made a very good living.

"I'll stay. I'm not that intrigued by the pending case anyway. I don't know much about your business, Sylvia, but I can promise to do the best I can." My stomach churned. I'd made another promise I didn't know if I could keep. Had I given in, or was it the excitement of a new challenge...sort of? "Since Gunner is going to be gone soon, I'll figure out meals. I might as well start by setting the table for supper." I turned to leave the sewing room, but turned back, "By the way, what are we eating?"

Kim and Sylvia laughed. "Sloppy Joes and chips with fruit salad," Kim said.

"Sounds good." I left with a lighter step until I thought of Gunner's attitude and my tense relationship with him and the distance between Kim and me.

Our dinner conversation gave me reason to hope. The events of the last three days in Chicago didn't seem as important as they once had. No thanks to me, the outcome would please the family, so my promise was fulfilled with or without me. During dinner, I focused on the conversation about the sewing Kim and Sylvia had scheduled for the days ahead. Gunner rarely talked about the book he was working on, but he was excited about resolving a plot point and giving the ending an unexpected twist.

They scattered after dinner, but I told the three of them I'd take care of the kitchen. I answered the house phone when the client with the cat costume called and scheduled a fitting for late the next afternoon. I left the kitchen with a slap on the counter. If I'd volunteered to make this my domain for a while, I'd keep it as organized as my desk.

When I went upstairs, Gunner was in bed watching a movie on his tablet. He'd left the bedside lamp on, so there was a glow of light in the room. I changed into my nightgown and sat in the comfy chair in the corner of the room and thought about all that had happened in such a short amount of time.

"Quit thinking, Charlotte, and come to bed and watch the movie with me. We need a good laugh." Gunner held out his hand.

He was right. I shut down my busy, worrying mind and joined him.

4

———

BY THE TIME I WENT DOWNSTAIRS THE NEXT MORNING, GUNNER
had the coffee brewing and eggs in the skillet. "I thought this
was my domain." I reached in the cupboard for one of Sylvia's
colorful mugs.

"I'll help with the cooking until I leave. That way, you'll be
able to pick up some tips on a few basic meals you can fix
while I'm gone, you know, favorites of Kim's and Mom's."

Everything about what he said, including his tone, made
me bristle. "I can read a cookbook, Gunner. And if you
remember, when Kim was growing up, I used to cook. You
didn't carry the whole load."

He kept his eyes on the frying pan. "Maybe so, but when
was the last time you bought groceries and made a real
meal?"

"Is that a challenge?"

His eyes twinkled when he said, "Hadn't planned it that
way, but I think it would be fun for me to see."

I held out my hand to seal the deal. "You're on." I transferred the plates of eggs Gunner handed to me to the table as
Sylvia and Kim entered the kitchen.

"What are you smiling about, Mom?"

"Your dad doesn't believe I can make a decent meal from scratch, so I'm about to prove him wrong."

Kim's amused smile filled her face. "With dessert?"

"Don't push your luck, Kim." Gunner sat in his chair and passed the plate of toast to Sylvia.

Kim poured tea for herself and Sylvia, but Gunner and I both wanted our coffee. As if Gunner and I disappeared, Sylvia and Kim began a conversation about a pumpkin costume they'd be working on. I slathered my toast with Sylvia's jam while I listened. Mmm. Maybe Sylvia would show me how to make that jam. Gunner smiled when I looked at him. He gave the impression he knew what I was thinking.

Gunner finished up first, and soon Kim and Sylvia left to begin their day. I began to clear the table. I poured myself another cup of coffee and looked at my new "office" and laughed. I grabbed a cookbook from those standing on the counter and paged to the table of contents and began flipping the pages back and forth between the recipes. My first meal might not look like perfect glossy photographs, but it would taste good, smell good, and have lots of color.

When the phone rang, I became the office assistant, and when the doorbell rang, I greeted Russ by name and reminded him who I was.

He grinned and handed me two boxes. "Good to meet you. See you soon, probably tomorrow." He hurried back to his truck and drove away.

I went into the sewing room to enter the new arrivals. Kim stepped over to show me how to open the computer program she'd named Client Data, which followed the same pattern as Sylvia's paper ledger.

Sylvia stopped sewing. "Who are they from?"

"Um, let's see." I held up one box. "This is from Carol Grayson, and the other is from Melissa Barrett. I'm not sure if they are for costumes or tailoring."

Sylvia nodded and returned to the piece she was sewing

together on the machine. Kim had returned to the cutting table and didn't look up. I saw three stacks of cut pieces on a nearby table. Yes, they'd been busy that morning.

I checked the clock on the wall. It was almost noon. Lunch! I ran to open the refrigerator and gasped. From gratitude. Gunner must have readied the tray of sandwiches while he made breakfast. Sitting next to the tray was a container of assorted fresh vegetables, cleaned and cut, ready for the table. He had attached a note to the cover on the sandwiches – tea for mom, milk for Kim, juice for me, and whatever you want. See you at noon. G

I took out the sandwiches to take the chill off of them and got the table ready. When Sylvia and Kim joined me, we finished the drinks. I waved at the plate of sandwiches. "Compliments of Gunner."

After eating so many meals alone for many years, sharing the table with my family was a wonderful change. Sylvia and Kim talked about their morning's work, but Gunner was closed mouth about his writing. He said he didn't want to scare the muse away.

I'd first heard him say that years ago when he was still freelancing. More than twenty-six years later, he was still talking about scaring the muse away. I listened to Sylvia and Kim speaking their language. They'd been doing that for a long time. I was the missing one, not them. I'd whoosh in with flashy success, but it was no wonder they had stopped being overly impressed, just like we all took for granted that Gunner would have yet another successful book. Maybe I could adjust to being just one part of this group, not its center, which I'd once flattered myself to believe was true. It never was, of course. Everyone in the family had successes and failures. For now, I'd just do my best with the little things that supported them.

Before Gunner went back to work, I asked him about supper.

"Don't worry about it. We've got enough soup and leftover sandwiches for another meal. We'll think up something different for tomorrow."

"Thank you, Gunner." I leaned forward and gave him a kiss. He wrapped his arms around me and gave me the kind of kiss I thought about while I was away. I finally pulled away, the heat rising on my neck. "We aren't exactly alone here."

Gunner laughed and let me go.

———

OVER THE NEXT FEW DAYS, I LEARNED MORE ABOUT COOKING from Gunner and the cookbooks and picked up some facts about sewing from Kim and Sylvia. They made it sound easy, but I knew that wasn't true. The phone continued to ring with sewing requests, and Sylvia's friends wanted to talk to her, mostly to see how she was doing. She'd asked me to tell them she was working hard and would get back to them at another time. I did as she asked and also got to meet many of her friends.

We seemed to be falling into a pleasant rhythm until Kim confided that she thought Sylvia was getting sick again. "She takes a lot of rest breaks now," she said. "I've tried to give her the easiest sewing projects, but..." She lifted her shoulders in defeat. "We'll never get all this sewing done before The Gathering in two weeks."

The Gathering was the town's Halloween celebration. Its official name, The Ghost and Goblin Gathering, was used in the advertising, but people in town shortened it to The Gathering. Costumes weren't required, but most of the kids were eager to dress up as one of their favorite action heroes or fairytale princesses. Many of the adults also dressed up, some in elaborate costumes, sewn by Sylvia—and now Kim. The parents supplied the treats and the games and had organized the event as a safer way to celebrate the holiday than going door to door.

I shrugged. "Is there anyone else you could bring in to help out?"

Kim put her hand on her hip and cocked her head. "Yep, you."

"Me?" I shook my head. "C'mon, I don't even know how to turn on a sewing machine, let alone operate it."

She swiped her hand across her forehead. "I'm not asking you to do that. But you could sew the buttons on or tack up the hems."

I stared at her long and hard. "By the way, how are *you* feeling? You don't need all this stress over the work that needs to be done."

A small smile crossed her face. "I don't think it's stressful. I love sewing, and each project is different. Gram and I make a great team." She planted her hand on her hip. "She promised these people she'd have their clothes and costumes done on time. I've seen Gram work all night, so a dress would be ready for a client."

"Sometimes, we make promises we shouldn't." I turned away, not wanting Kim to ask questions. Neither of us spoke for a moment. "Okay, I'll do what I can."

She bent forward to give me the kind of hug only a pregnant woman could do. "Thanks, Mom. I'll tell Gram you'll help."

That evening I cleaned up the kitchen after supper and got it ready for morning. Sylvia sat in a chair with a witch's costume across her lap. She'd already attached three buttons. More buttons were in the bowl next to her on the table. The floor lamp shone brightly from over her shoulder. "Pull up a chair. I'll show you how I want these done, then you can do the rest. My eyes are tired tonight."

"It's no wonder. You and Kim have been working overtime every day since you came home from the hospital."

"I promised they'd be done, and I'll work night and day to keep that promise."

Oh, Mom. You and Sylvia were cut from the same cloth, and Kim and I are following in your footsteps.

After giving me what she no doubt believed were precise directions for sewing on the buttons, Sylvia watched while I made my first attempt. When I finished, I showed her what I'd done.

"That's fine, Charlotte, but the hat is upside down." She pointed to the three witch's hat buttons she'd sewn on. "See? Yours isn't like these?"

Sure enough. The buttons were triangular shaped witch's hats, with a pointed top. Did it matter if the pointed tip of all the hats weren't positioned the same way? Apparently so. Sylvia grabbed the scissors and cut the threads I'd just sewn.

"Let me correct my mistake." I took the costume back and threaded the needle again.

Sylvia watched as I sewed two more buttons on under her watchful eye. I must have done it right this time because she stood and gave my shoulder a quick squeeze and left the room. "See you in the morning."

I didn't look at the clock when I finished attaching the last of the twenty buttons, but I could have shouted for joy when I put the garment on the cutting table, and all the hat buttons were in a perfect row.

———

GOING ON RENEWED ENERGY, I BEAT GUNNER TO THE KITCHEN the next morning and had the coffee and toast going when he arrived. I'd put the egg carton on the counter as part of the routine to start our day. There was no arguing with Gunner. He insisted we needed a hearty breakfast. All of us, every day.

When he came into the kitchen, he headed for the coffee pot and grabbed a mug and filled it.

"It's time you show me your tricks for making your perfect eggs." I'd been eating them for years, but never thought about asking him how to make them myself.

"It's not exactly a secret trick. Just warm the pan, crack the eggs into a bowl, and pour them into the pan."

"Really? Why dirty a bowl? Can't you just crack them right into the pan?"

Gunner responded with a smug shrug. "If that's how you want to do it, be my guest. But, if you want *perfect* eggs, they all have to hit the pan at the same time. Otherwise, the first egg overcooks, and the last one is still raw. The trick is all in the timing."

Why was I volunteering to do this? I momentarily forgot. But I nudged Gunner aside and began to crack the eggs into a bowl. Two of the yolks broke.

He peered over my shoulder. "Don't hit the egg on the bowl so hard."

I turned and gave him a pointed look.

"Okay, okay. I'll finish the toast."

I started over, and a few minutes later, the pan was filled with perfectly cooked eggs. Except for those I broke, which I'd eat. I puffed out my chest a little. My first breakfast in my new job with my made-up title, family assistant. Kim and Sylvia took their places at the table and dug into the eggs and toast.

"Not bad, Mom," Kim said after her first bite. "So, what's for lunch? You know how it is. All I can think about is food."

"And here I thought it was sewing that filled your head." A smile escaped before Sylvia dipped her head.

Kim made quick work of breakfast and got to her feet. "Time for us to begin another day, Gram." She put her hands on the back of her hips and arched her back. "I'm going to sit and sew this morning. I think I overdid it yesterday with all the standing and cutting."

Gunner added more coffee to his cup. "There's a package

of hamburger patties in the fridge for lunch. Best check to see if they thawed out overnight." He left the kitchen with a wave.

Suddenly, I was alone in the kitchen. I thought I'd done a good job with breakfast, but now I had to think about lunch? Of course, while I was gone, Gunner had been cooking three meals a day for three adults, one of whom was pregnant, so maybe after two weeks, it was all part of his routine.

Looking at the jobs I'd just finished, it took two tries to sew a button on right, and second, I'd broken two egg yolks by not being careful enough. Somehow, my successes in the court-room had tainted my ability to focus on doing small jobs well.

I prepared the kitchen for lunch with renewed focus. I looked for ways to minimize my stress of lunchtime coming on the heels of breakfast. And why was I finding this so upsetting? I thought of Gunner having prepared a tray of sandwiches while he made breakfast. I could do that too and keep my ego in check.

Mid-morning, Kim returned to the kitchen by telling Sylvia she was going for water. "Mom, Gram told me she is going to rest for a while instead of having lunch."

At first, I wanted to run upstairs to tell Gunner about Kim's concern. I got it. Sylvia needed to pace herself and rest. But she also needed to eat. "You go back to your sewing. I'll talk to Gram." I sounded calmer and more in control than I felt.

Sylvia had left the door to her bedroom open, so I walked in. She opened her eyes when I pulled a small chair to her bedside and sat. "Kim tells me you're not interested in lunch today."

"I'm too tired right now, but pudding sounds good for later. I've got some in the cupboard."

Did I hear her correctly? Sylvia had premade food in her house? I wasn't surprised to see packaged food in her cupboard now that Gunner was doing the shopping. But when had Sylvia begun eating pudding from plastic cups? "I thought those might have been for Kim or Gunner as a midnight snack." I smiled when she took my hand.

"For me, too." She closed her eyes. "Later." I was about to leave when she added, "Good job on the buttons."

Touched that she'd think to mention it, I said, "Thank you." I closed her door when I left.

When we sat down to eat, Kim was eager to talk about Sylvia and the sewing. "We're still getting interrupted way too much."

I noted the strain in her voice, but I wasn't sure there was much I could do. I'd tried to field the calls, but sometimes, well, most of the time, I needed to interrupt Kim or Sylvia for an answer.

"Your mother is doing her best with the calls, Kim." Gunner swallowed a bite of coleslaw and then challenged Kim. "Would you be able to manage briefs and depositions and evidence if you had no training?"

"Sorry, Mom," Kim said, grimacing, "but I know how important this sewing is for Gram, and I'm the only one that can help her."

"Oh, I don't about that." I told them about Sylvia's lesson on sewing buttons. Kim and Gunner laughed when I told them that Sylvia cut off my first attempt and made me redo it. "I'm sure there's more I can do. Just keep delaying any projects that don't have to be done by Halloween. You said a few clients ordered Christmas outfits."

Kim nodded. "Mrs. Sommers and Julia Campshire." She polished off her second burger while I kept talking. She wasn't kidding about being hungry all the time. "You logged in most of the projects, so make a list by priority. I'll let callers know Sylvia can't do any last minute costumes this year."

I felt more in control when I saw the problem and had a solution. "Leave the dishes. I'll do them later."

I left Kim and Gunner at the table and grabbed a spoon and napkin, and found a container of vanilla pudding.

Sylvia heard me arrive. "I'll eat it now." She boosted herself up and leaned against the headboard. "My hand is tired from sewing. Will you open it for me?"

"Absolutely." I did as she asked and opened the napkin for her to put under her chin. "We were talking at lunch, and the consensus is that we take in no new Halloween sewing projects. I'll handle the phone calls so it'll be on my shoulders, not yours. Kim is going through the orders this afternoon, and we're going to streamline the projects by grouping similar requests together rather than doing them as they arrive. Is that okay with you?"

I had never spoken to Sylvia in that tone of authority or ever presumed I knew enough about her sewing business to make such suggestions. But her situation, which included Gunner, Kim, and me, was different than it had been before.

"You can bring me Kim's list. I'll have a look. I'm sure I've sewn for some of them for many years."

"Of course. I didn't mean to imply we were taking over," I said. "But Kim will need more rest as the weeks go on, and you can't continue at this pace."

She scraped the inside of the container with the spoon to eat every last bit of pudding and then handed me the empty cup. "Thank you for being honest and taking charge." She laid back and closed her eyes.

"You rest. And don't worry. I'll check on you a little later." I closed her door when I left.

When I returned to the kitchen, Kim had the list in her hand. "This is worse than I thought, Mom. When the boxes came in one or two at a time, I didn't think much about it, but, whew, there's a lot to do." She put her hand on her stomach.

I pulled out a chair for her. "Sit. It won't do anyone any good—especially you and Sylvia—if you let the sewing overwhelm you."

She rubbed her stomach and grinned. "The baby is kicking more now than before."

"Normal, but it can be jolting. Have you seen a doctor since you've been here?" I'd ventured into unspoken territory and was surprised Kim didn't leave the room.

She nodded. "I have appointments scheduled up to the delivery date. Everything is progressing normally, the doctor's exact words." She looked back at the pages she'd printed. "About these."

"I'd like to see them." Sylvia made her way to the table and sat next to Kim.

Sylvia used her finger to go down the pages of orders. "You're right, Charlotte. We'll be lucky to get all these done before The Gathering. And I don't want to disappoint anyone. You know how I feel about promises."

"What do you suggest?" I waited for Sylvia to give us her opinion, but began to brush stray crumbs off the table.

"Do you think Barbara would help if I called her?" Sylvia asked. "Sewing is sewing whether it's a costume or a liner for a basket, and she's been doing all kinds of sewing for her crafts."

"You think my sister can help? Isn't her kind of sewing different from yours?" I'd never thought of Barbara coming down to help and was surprised Sylvia had.

"Sewing is sewing," Sylvia repeated with a smile. After seeing the list of projects, Sylvia was certain she and Kim would never finish the orders that had arrived. "I'll call her now."

Sylvia went to the small desk in the kitchen and opened her personal phone directory and located the number. She sat in the chair to enter Barbara's number on her house phone. Suddenly, her face brightened. "Barbara. I'm so glad I reached you. It's Sylvia. How are you doing?"

A couple of seconds later, Sylvia said. "Oh, yes, thank you. Kim told me she called you. I'm feeling much better."

"I need your help, or rather *we* do. I hope you'll say yes."

Sylvia listened and grinned. "Yes, by *we*, I mean Kim and me. Gunner has been here for a couple of weeks, and Charlotte arrived a couple of days ago. Too many costume orders have come in for Kim and me to get done in the next two weeks. The Gathering is the last Saturday of October."

Her grin widened. "That's what I said. Here, I'll let you talk to Charlotte. She's handling the logistics for me until the end of the year. See you soon. And thanks."

Having only heard one side to their conversation, I filled Barbara in about the sewing and assured her she could stay in the one empty bedroom upstairs. Barbara agreed to come for the weekend. She'd bring her own sewing machine because she could sew faster on a machine she was familiar with. Barbara lived in Superior, Wisconsin, near the Minnesota border. Her accounting and tax career had taken her to settle in many different towns over the years.

When I hung up the phone, Gunner joined us. Sylvia, Kim, and I ended up talking over each other about all that had happened just since breakfast.

"It's only one extra person, but I'll pitch in to help with meals if you need it," he said to me. "I can do a grocery run and make a pot of soup."

"Okay, let's start the list," I said. "Looks like we're hunkering down and going into production."

They all looked at me as if seeing me for the first time. "Hey, don't look at me like I'm a stranger. I do know a thing or two about organization, you know."

"To Mom," Kim said with a laugh in her voice. She raised her half-full glass of milk.

5

By Friday, the fourth bedroom upstairs was ready for Barbara. When she pulled into the driveway, I ran from the house to greet her. We hugged and laughed as if it had been years since we'd seen each other. Actually, it had been over a year, but that was because I had back to back cases that kept me away. I'd not even been home much, let alone had time to visit Barbara.

Barbara stopped cold when Kim stood on the porch. Oops. I suppose I should have called Barbara privately and told her about the baby. Or someone should have, like Kim herself. But she'd had made it plain the baby was her responsibility, so I assumed she'd meant telling her family was for her, and only her, to do.

"Oh, Kim, you look wonderful," Barbara said, recovering from her surprise enough to sound normal. "When's the baby due?"

"Christmas." Kim turned. "Gram's waiting, so come on in." She held the door open for us and gave Barbara a one-arm hug.

Sylvia was in the sewing room when we went inside. She greeted Barbara with open arms and thanked her repeatedly for coming to help. I could see some signs of Sylvia's stress disappearing from her face. Ever since Gunner and I married, Sylvia had generously included my single sister in family events and holiday celebrations.

Our talking and laughter brought Gunner down from his writing to say hello. He unloaded Barbara's car and put the suitcase by the stairs and her sewing machine in the sewing room.

Sylvia waved off Barbara's offer to begin immediately. Instead, we gathered in the kitchen, where Gunner was adding a leaf to give the five of us a little more room at the table. I started the kettle for tea, and Gunner brought out a bottle of wine he had chilling. Sylvia told him to use her best wine glasses. "You may find some dust on them."

I couldn't remember when my whole family had last been together, but I pushed that thought away. It wasn't the time to think about regrets.

The casserole warmed while I finished our salad and listened to the others catch up. Barbara seemed to lift everyone's spirits. I'd missed being with them last Christmas, so I heard about the Christmas movie marathon they'd had. Apparently, they'd convinced Sylvia to open their gifts on Christmas Eve morning. The good mood lasted through the meal. Then Sylvia and Kim led Barbara to the sewing room and its lengthy project list. Gunner helped me right the kitchen and prepare for morning.

By the time we finished, Sylvia and Kim had gone to their rooms. Gunner had taken Barbara's suitcase upstairs. He planned to write for a few more hours. Barbara and I enjoyed another glass of wine in front of the fireplace. We sat on the couch facing each other. "Tell me about Kim and the baby," Barbara said.

"I know as much as you do." I shrugged. "She didn't call me about her pregnancy. Apparently, she didn't tell Gunner either until she got here. That surprises me with the two of them being so close." I fingered the fabric on the cushion.

"What about her boyfriend?"

"She says he's chosen not to be involved." Lowering my voice, I added, "Frankly, with her reluctance to talk about the baby, I'm not sure she has given her future much thought. It seems she took a leave of absence and came here."

"Really? Maybe while I'm here, I can get her to open up a little. She's happy to be here that's for sure." Barbara tucked one leg under her.

"And how it is that you can come on such short notice?" I asked.

Barbara laughed. "Are you being the big sister?"

"Oh, maybe. You know I care about you. I miss you, too. I'm tired of being gone all the time when I should be enjoying my family." I shook my head. "But back to you."

"I'm not going to renew my contract with the tax firm," she said, staring at the fire. "Right now, I'm living on vacation and comp time until the end of the year. I get to do that because they let me bank my leave time for the last two years."

It wouldn't be the first time she got restless and looked for a new place to start fresh. "Where will you go?"

"I'm thinking about doing contract work like you do, but for corporations. The trend right now is outsourcing, but I don't want to travel like you do. There are a couple of big businesses in Superior I want to contact soon." Barbara put her empty glass on the floor next to her chair.

"The traveling was exciting, especially in the beginning," I said, "but I'm finding hotel living to be lonely and sterile. It used to be the rush of winning made up for it, but not so much now. Sad to say, but I don't have any real friends after all the years of traveling."

Barbara reached out to touch my hand. "Sounds like burnout to me. When was the last time you and Gunner had a real vacation or even an evening out?"

I couldn't look her in the eye. She'd probably guessed it had been too long ago for me to remember. I stood up. "More wine?"

"None for me." After two back-to-back yawns, Barbara was ready for bed. Just as well. I assured her there'd be little time for rest the next day.

————

THE PHONE STARTED RINGING AS SOON AS WE FINISHED A French toast breakfast. I'd put out the local maple syrup and Sylvia's jam, plus a bowl of sliced fruit. It seemed like we all gathered steam during the night when our conversation picked up where we'd left off the evening before. It was a wonderful sound to hear.

I tucked the phone under my chin so I could use both hands to fill the dishwasher and clean the frying pans. I told the woman that Sylvia was unable to take any more costume orders. She begged, pleaded, and even offered a ridiculously large payment for a rush order. My politeness quotient was almost exhausted when the lady relented by telling me she would call earlier next year.

Two more calls followed the first. I didn't have an esti-mated finish date for either order, so I made a note to have that included on Kim's sheets. I promised a return call.

I brought a pitcher of water and glasses to the sewing room. They were deep in a discussion of different sewing machines and things like pre-wound bobbins, needle sizes for different fabrics, and the pros and cons of different makes and models of machines. I had no idea what they were talking about, so I left them to it.

On Sunday afternoon, Barbara told us she'd come back the following Friday and stay through the next week to sew and attend The Gathering. She'd told me about the weeks of vacation she'd accumulated working for a family-owned tax office but never felt that she belonged there.

The smile on her face when she left told me she had enjoyed her time with her family. It was hard to see her drive away on such a beautiful October day. Instead of going right back to the chores ahead, I grabbed my jacket to take a walk along the country road, not too far from Sylvia's house. The maple trees were in full color, and the bright gold leaves of the birch trees highlighted their shaggy white bark.

"Charlotte, wait for me," Gunner called from behind. He walked fast to catch up.

"Something wrong?" My stomach tightened. With Sylvia recently ill and Kim's pregnancy so far along, I had them on my mind constantly.

"No. Needed to get out and move around. I've been sitting for days."

"And the book?" Sometimes asking Gunner about his writing made him defensive, or, at other times, excited to share his latest ideas. I could never tell from his expression, so I rarely asked anymore.

"We haven't talked about my writing for a long time, or ... about anything, for that matter." His tone was flat, matter-of-fact.

"I tried, but..."

Gunner waved me off. "Water under the bridge. Let's look ahead. Walks like this one would be a good place to start."

I stopped and turned to Gunner. "Have you been thinking about us too?"

He cocked his head and flashed a flirtatious smile. "Maybe. Or maybe I miss my wife."

He wrapped his arms around me, and his lips almost touched mine.

"Sorry to interrupt, Gunner." Lester Grant stood on his front porch. He was Charlotte's nearest neighbor. His face had changed little since the last time I saw him, but his shoulders were bent forward and his body smaller, almost frail.

"Hello, Lester. Something you need?" Gunner kept me near his side as we approached the porch.

"Not really," he said, shaking his head, "but would you give Sylvia this jar of honey? I heard she's been ill, and this might help her feel better."

"Why, thanks, Lester," Gunner said, approaching the porch. "We'll all enjoy it. Kim is here, too, and do you remember my wife, Charlotte?"

Lester nodded. "Been a long time."

While we stood there, a younger man, Lester's son, I figured by his resemblance, joined us. "And this is John. He's moving to Willow Birch to help with the farm and the bees. He's a carpenter, so if you need something done, he's the man to call."

Gunner reached over the railing to shake John's hand. "And my wife, Charlotte."

"I'll be staying with Sylvia and our daughter while Gunner is away on his book tour, so I'm glad to meet you." I nodded to both men. "You should stop in if you get a chance. I know Sylvia would enjoy it."

"Thank you. Maybe this weekend, but we'll give you a call first. I know how busy Sylvia is with her sewing this time of year." Lester gave us a quick wave.

"A break to see some friends would be good for all of us." Gunner held up the jar of honey. "And, thanks again."

We made our way back to the house as dusk approached. "Can I have a walking day tomorrow?" Gunner finished the kiss we'd started before we went inside.

I hesitated. A bad habit I'd developed.

Gunner sighed impatiently. "Just say yes, Charlotte."

"Yes."

Someone had left a small lamp on in the sewing room for our return, but neither Sylvia nor Kim was waiting for us. I assumed they had gone off to their rooms to be alone for a while. Kim rarely mentioned her old friends, but maybe she caught up with them during her evenings by herself. "I'll ready the kitchen for morning. Do you want a sandwich or some soup?"

"Just some cheese and crackers and a cup of soup." He suggested a few short cuts that would make the morning rush less hectic for me. It was obvious he had tried different routines before finding the one that worked best.

We ended the day and started our evening arm in arm. A rarity. And I wanted more of it.

―――

THE FOLLOWING WEEK SYLVIA AND KIM SPENT MANY HOURS IN the sewing room. I'd see them at lunch, which gave them a break, and I more or less insisted they rest for a bit after they ate.

"So bossy," Sylvia said, smiling as she left the kitchen, but her tone was light and cheerful.

I spent the afternoon packaging finished projects for shipping or calling local clients to come for a fitting. It wasn't unusual for packages to be delivered and picked up at the same time by Russ from UPS and Gail, the FedEx driver. I got to know each better as one day blended into the next.

On Thursday evening, Barbara arrived to spend the week with us and join us at The Gathering. "After seeing all these costumes, I definitely want to go to the party."

―――

THE DAY OF THE GHOSTS AND GOBLINS GATHERING ARRIVED, and we were ready to go to the afternoon party, now in its tenth year at the Community Center. Like many events, The

Gathering had started small and grown into a party that signaled the beginning of the holiday season.

The five of us and our baskets of treats needed two cars. Kim joked that it was six of us, so maybe she needed two seats. She'd decided that a pregnant ghost was the best costume for her.

"Easy for bathroom breaks," she said with a laugh.

Sylvia had her fairy godmother dress from last year, so she was set to go. Gunner had been watching a documentary series on Caribbean pirates, so all he wanted was a simple eye patch and a big silver sword. We talked him into adding a few gold chain necklaces for fun.

Barbara and I had driven to Green Bay one evening to see what we could scare up in the way of costumes. I didn't want anything elaborate, and I didn't want Sylvia or Kim to think they needed to make me one. Barbara immediately found a red cape and golden wig. She'd be Little Red Riding Hood.

That left me. I went through the rack twice before settling on a prairie dress with a matching hat. Just then, I thought of Betsy Ross sewing the flag. I was sure Sylvia had scraps of red, white, and blue fabric I could use, but I wouldn't have to do any actual sewing, so no one would know I couldn't sew a stitch.

Each year a Gathering host or hostess greeted the party goers. Last year Sylvia had been given the honor, and Gunner had told me she played the role well by giving each person, child, and adult, a fairy wish when she tapped their shoulders with her wand.

As we neared the entrance, I saw George Pearson—Judge Pearson—dressed in his tuxedo with his Halloween fabric cummerbund and matching bow tie standing at the door. Sylvia never mentioned him being the host that day. I wondered if that was on purpose. I ducked behind Sylvia and Kim, hoping to avoid him. Maybe, he wouldn't see me.

No luck.

"And who is this all dressed in her finery?" he asked in a booming voice. "The lawyer who ran from my courtroom a few weeks ago?"

I hadn't told my family that the case I lost in Chicago was tried in Judge Pearson's court. I'd known Kim and Sylvia had met him years ago, but I'd had no idea how involved he was in Willow Birch.

All conversation halted, and those nearby moved closer to hear more.

"Hello. I'm surprised to see you here. I hear this is quite the party. At least Sylvia says so." I spoke quickly and had to fight the urge to blend into the large room.

"It's for the kids, so what's not to enjoy?" He lightly touched my arm. "Before you leave tonight, please find me."

The line behind us pushed forward, forcing Gunner up against my back. My feet might as well have been stuck in concrete. "Charlotte, let's move along," Gunner whispered in my ear.

All I could think about were Pearson's last words. Why would he want to see me? Now, I wanted to leave altogether. Forget the party. I'd go hide in Sylvia's house. Or, it occurred to me that Ben Davis might have contacted him for some reason. Great, now my failure could be paraded in front of my family and everyone else in town.

Gunner and I spotted Kim and Barbara, who'd staked out a table and arranged our baskets to form a centerpiece around the carved pumpkin. Sylvia was "holding court" with a group of small children all dressed in ladybug costumes that made their group easy to keep track of.

I chose a chair that put my back to the room. I thought the less I was seen, the better, but I needn't have worried. No one was paying attention to me. The room was soon full of boisterous kids and their equally loud parents. I relaxed and turned my chair around to become part of the party.

The windows of the Community Center had been covered

to give a darkened feel to the room. Artificial trees in the corners were strung with white and orange miniature lights. Along one wall, a long table was laden with finger foods for the taking.

Lester and John joined us. Lester was dressed in his beekeeper's suit, complete with the mesh head gear. John wore his carpenter's belt and had stuck a pair of gloves in his back pockets. John pulled up a chair next to Barbara, where there was an open area. After introductions, they began talking as if no one else was in the room.

Well, well.

When the children's parade was announced, the adults stood in a ring around the room with their treats ready to drop into the children's bags. I watched Sylvia as she bent forward and talked to each child as if no one else was in the room before she gave them her treat. Barbara stood and helped Kim.

Gunner nudged my elbow when a young boy dressed in a worn out T-shirt and jeans too short for his height with patched knees stopped in front of me. "Give him two. That's not a costume."

My heart went out to the young boy. I wanted to give him my entire basket of treats and toys. "Do you have any brothers or sisters?"

"Mom's home with the younger ones." He twisted his head to look around the room. "Sheryl's here somewhere. She's my older sister."

"Take a couple more, but be sure to share when you get home."

His eyes got big. "Thank you." He looked back when the line moved ahead. I waved.

"Gunner, who is that?"

"Alex Anderson. Lost his dad about two years ago, and the family's having a rough go of it."

I usually wasn't so taken by kids, but something about Alex pulled at my heart. I wanted to ask Gunner more about the Anderson situation, but a new group of children stepped up for their treats.

By late afternoon the children had expended their energy with the games and bartering their treats with one another. The band was packing up. The table of finger foods was almost empty. Kim and Sylvia had already left with Lester, who offered them a lift home after the parade. Barbara and John said they were headed for the coffee shop in town. Gunner left and came back with two cups of hot apple cider for us. A few minutes later, George Pearson joined us at our table. Gunner took off his eye patch.

"Wonderful party," he said. "Lori, my granddaughter, gone now, would have enjoyed being here. She loved Willow Birch when we came in the summers." There was wistfulness in his voice.

"We all had a good time," I said. "Too bad it's only one day of the year for all the work the community does to put it together. Kim told me about your granddaughter. I'm sorry for your loss."

"But you could bring some meaning to her death, Charlotte. This community needs a good lawyer now that David McClure suffered a stroke and lives in a nursing home in Green Bay. Lori wanted to be a lawyer and work in a small town like Willow Birch."

"But I'm not—"

He waved me off. "Why don't you think about changing your direction now? Sylvia and Kim could use your help. So does this community."

"Well, obviously, I'd need to think about making a big change like that. And talk with Gunner." I reached over to take his hand. "All I can promise is that I'll give it some thought."

Why had I promised even that? When would I learn?

Judge Pearson gave me a long look, filled with meaning I didn't comprehend. "Sometimes promises lead us down the wrong road and make it pretty hard to backtrack."

I bowed my head to acknowledge his words. "I'd be the first to agree, Judge."

"Call me George. I'm not a judge when I come to Willow Birch."

I smiled. "Got it. Do you come to town often?"

"Not as often as I'd like, but I'll move here when I retire. I've got friends here who want nothing more than to have another person at the poker table." George got to his feet and said goodnight. I watched him make his way to the door, stopping at each of the small groups remaining to thank them for coming. He was more than a host that evening. He was a member of the community.

Gunner also watched George make his rounds. "Well, did you see that coming?"

"Never," I said. "Obviously, I can blow the whole thing off. First of all, we don't even live in Wisconsin, and I'm not licensed here. Besides, I'm a criminal defense lawyer. I don't care much about wills or estates or real estate."

"Except for the type of law you want to practice, everything else is easy enough to deal with. Who says we have to live in Minnesota now? I don't need to be there. You rarely have cases there. I'm sure Mom would love to have us closer."

I waved to George when we left the building. After grazing on finger foods all afternoon, Gunner and I decided to skip dinner. During the drive home—when had I begun to think of Sylvia's house as home, I wondered?—I asked Gunner about the Anderson family. After he filled in some details, I talked about the government-run programs to help families in that kind of trouble. "I've seen Social Services in action, Gunner."

Gunner shrugged. "Maybe so, but I'm too busy to get involved right now. The school should know how to steer them in the right direction."

"Could be, but we don't know what's being done. Are we going to watch this family end up homeless and the children go hungry?"

Gunner grinned. "Sounds like you want to get involved. Maybe make sure the family gets what it needs."

I tapped his shoulder. "Don't go volunteering me, my friend. I'll think about how I could help. And while I'm thinking, I'll consider what George suggested. I'll have to call him back one way or the other."

When Gunner pulled into the driveway of Sylvia's house, we saw Barbara and John in her car. I hadn't seen that big a smile on Barbara's face in a long time, so for fun, I rapped on the window and waved.

Later, I noticed Sylvia's godmother costume on the cutting table when I went looking for Sylvia and Kim. Apparently, they'd gone to their rooms. I did my nightly walk through the house. The unfamiliar sounds in the night had thrown me when I first arrived, so I'd taken to making sure all the doors were locked and the lights turned off before heading upstairs. In the back of my mind, I'd wondered if it was safe for Sylvia to be alone on the main floor. How would she call for help if she needed it? Barbara and John were still outside, so I left the door unlocked for them.

6

THE NEXT MORNING, I TOLD GUNNER I NEEDED TO DRIVE TO Minneapolis to check on our condo and pick up some winter clothes for both of us. Buying new wardrobes made no sense when we had full closets at home. I still had court suits packed away in the luggage I'd brought. "I promise you I'll be gone no more than three days."

Gunner frowned. "That's cutting it close. I'm flying to New York the day after you get back. But, still, since you're going, I want my charcoal suit and that blue tie I like."

"I'll make it back," I said, patting his shoulder. "I'll go tell our sewing ladies I'll be on my way in the morning."

"You're leaving, Mom?" Kim met me in the doorway of the kitchen.

"No...well, yes. But not for a case. I'm doing a quick trip home to pick up some winter clothes for your dad and me."

Kim took her regular chair at the table. "That's good. I'm glad you're here to help us, especially with Dad leaving soon." There was a worried look on her face.

"I promise I'll be here." I almost took my words back as I thought about my last promises.

———

MINNEAPOLIS WAS A THREE HUNDRED MILE CAR TRIP FROM Willow Birch, which was about the same time it took to listen to the audio version of Gunner's last release. I'd read the print book, but I also liked to listen to his writing. Gunner loosely used real life police cases as a basis for his writing, but he changed them so much no one would be able to identify the case. He added characters and changed locations and other details that made his books entertaining. This story ended with the police discovering a satellite photo of a car in the driveway of the home of the murdered sisters. The clear image of the license plate was the evidence they needed to solve the case.

Could fiction be that close to real life? Missing the same kind of evidence had led to my downfall in court. It gave me a little chill to think of it.

I reached the condo within minutes of the story ending, so I sat in the car and listened until the narrator read the last line. While I listened, I noticed the cream exterior of the condo complex had been painted a soft gray. Seeing it, I recalled Gunner had mentioned an extra maintenance fee for an exterior upgrade, but I'd forgotten to ask.

A fragrant smell greeted me when I opened the door. No one had been there since Gunner had gone to Willow Birch to be with his mother two weeks ago. I lit the jar candle on the kitchen counter to make sure the pleasant scent wouldn't fade. The business card for the cleaning service was dated last week, and the latest mail was in neat stacks next to the candle. I scanned the envelopes but found nothing that needed our immediate attention. Postal receipts were next to the mail, so apparently, Gunner had arranged for someone to forward our mail to him in Willow Birch.

I walked through the living room, the den, and two of the three bedrooms. The master suite was as I remembered. Sadly, all in all, it looked more like a *House Beautiful* layout than someone's home. Even our personal pictures looked out of place.

I sat on the edge of the bed, and George's—and Gunner's—suggestion that we move to Willow Birch came to mind. But if I gave up my cases and no longer took on clients all over the country, would there be enough work to support a full-time practice? And would I find the work challenging?

I needed more information, so I wandered back into the kitchen and retrieved my phone and George's business card. It wouldn't hurt to call him. I entered the number before I could change my mind.

He answered on the second ring. "Hello, Charlotte. Did you call to say yes?"

"Judge—oops, George—I'm in Minneapolis getting winter clothes for Gunner and me." I walked to the living room windows and glanced outside while I gathered my thoughts. "I was thinking about your suggestion while I drove, but no, I haven't made a decision. I need answers. For one thing, do you think the practice would give me enough challenging work? I mean, I'm not exactly longing to file wills or close real estate sales."

He hesitated a minute like he always did in court. "I don't know what you consider challenging, but I can tell you it would be satisfying. You'd file wills and handle some real estate, most likely, but your clients would be your neighbors, people in Willow Birch. They'd be people you'd get to know."

"Why don't you retire from the bench and start a legal business of your own?"

He laughed.

"Don't laugh. I'm serious."

"When I retire, I'm going fishing and leave all that legal stuff to you young people."

"Could I count on you for help if I ever needed it?"

"Does that mean you've already decided?"

"Ha. No way." Keeping my voice light, I added, "I'm just visualizing an office filled with clients. I might need help handling all the business."

"You keep thinking that way. Call me again if you need to." He paused. "This is important, Charlotte, for you and Willow Birch."

When we ended the call, I stared out the window and thought about George. He was a respected judge. I always found him honest and fair. Neither side could say he showed favoritism. So, I'd be fine working with him, or even having him work for me, depending on my decision.

I sent a text to Gunner and Kim, letting them know I'd arrived safely. I spent the afternoon opening closets and cupboards and wondering how we'd accumulated so much stuff. For supper, I ordered delivery from my favorite Thai restaurant. That was fine, but food was on my mind again when I awakened. Thanks to Gunner, I no longer got by on coffee in the morning. I dressed quickly and went to the coffee shop nearby and ordered an omelet with the works, and then two sandwiches, chips, and bottles of juice to go.

Back at the condo, the refrigerator had a bare, hollow sound when I put my lunch and drinks inside. I imagined the cleaning service had removed everything Gunner had left when he was called to Willow Birch.

I piled up Gunner's clothes first, putting coats, hats, gloves, and scarves on the bed. I dragged his snow boots from the back corner of the closet. Then I grabbed a suitcase from our collection of luggage and filled it with slacks and jeans, sweaters and flannel shirts, his favorite everyday clothes. I tossed in an extra belt.

I filled another suitcase with the same kind of clothes for me but added a couple of wool suits and matching heels. My classic suits and dress slacks didn't really go out of style, and I'd been taking the same pieces across the country from job to job for years. I didn't worry about having a different look every day.

By noon the suitcases were packed and stood by the front door. I hadn't thought I'd end up sorting through the Christmas boxes, but I wanted to have some of our favorite ornaments on Sylvia's tree this year. Maybe Kim would want a few of her favorites so she could tell the baby about them. There were so many boxes to go through before I found what I wanted. I'd forgotten how many ornaments and other decorations we'd packed away.

Whether I was sorting clothes or ornaments, I couldn't stop mulling over George's idea. It kept building and leading me in different directions. There'd be no reason to keep the condo if we moved to Willow Birch. We'd have to find a new place to live. And would Kim want to live with us when she had the baby? Were we ready to have her back home with us? Was she going to return to her job? That's what she said, but it was hard to picture her packing up and leaving Sylvia. Sadly, Kim rarely talked about the baby coming, and Gunner and I didn't push the conversation.

Since Gunner was aware of George's idea, he knew I was considering the possibility of changing the way I practiced, maybe giving up the big cases that kept me away for so long. Some cases took years to prepare, and if we were lucky, never went to trial at all. I never asked him about moving to Willow Birch. But it wouldn't hurt to forge ahead and gather information. When I called the condo office, I asked the manager if they had a list of people interested in owning a unit. She didn't hesitate. "We do have a long list, and right now, prices are holding high because of the demand. Are you...uh, wanting to sell?"

"No. This is a fact-finding call," I said in my professional voice.

"All right. And would you mind telling Mr. Wilson I've pre-ordered his next book? His last book about the sisters kept me reading late into the night. Do you think he'd autograph my book when he returns?"

"I'm sure Gunner would be happy to sign your book." I disconnected before she asked more questions about him and the call became social.

That evening after enjoying my second sandwich, I called Gunner to be sure I'd packed his favorite things, including the charcoal suit and blue tie. I told him I'd be on the road early in the morning.

"Travel safe, Charlotte. We miss your cooking." His laughter warmed my heart.

My cooking *had* improved some since taking most of the cooking off Gunner's hands so he could focus on his book. But we all knew what I produced was a far cry from the tasty dishes Gunner made.

The next day I crossed the Mississippi River into Wisconsin before noon. I was west of Wausau when steam burst from under the hood of my car. Startled, but still in control, I turned on my signal light and pulled onto the shoulder of the road and turned off the engine.

Now what?

I got out and was about to lift the hood of the car when a pick-up truck pulled up behind my car. A young man got out and walked toward me.

"Lady, you got trouble?" He put his hands in the pockets of his jeans.

"Appears so. Any suggestions?"

"Smells like antifreeze. Must be the radiator or a hose."

"Can I drive it to the next exit?"

He smiled. "No way. You'll burn the engine if you do."

"Well, I guess there's nothing to do but call road service and wait. Thank you for stopping."

"Um... my friend has a garage nearby. I could call him."

I didn't know this man or his friend, but I wouldn't know the driver of the roadside help truck either. I considered calling Gunner, but what would he do? I relied on my experience reading people and decided that the young man had no ulterior motives.

"Thanks. That would be helpful."

He pulled a phone from his pocket and called his friend. "Be about ten minutes for him to get here."

I reached into my car for my coat. The sun was offering little warmth, and each time clouds passed over it, I felt a chill.

The young man and I chatted enough to exchange some basic information. He worked for a local construction company and was en route from one site to another. He waved when he saw his friend's truck approach.

Within minutes my car was loaded, and I was riding in the wrecker. I had a few zings of anxiety travel through me, but they departed quickly when we arrived at Joe's Auto Repair. It only took a few minutes for the mechanic to determine that, yes, there was a split in one of the radiator hoses.

"I don't have this part in stock," the mechanic said. "The quickest I can get it is tomorrow morning if you want me to fix it."

"Of course." How else would it get repaired? No sense towing it somewhere else. "Is there a motel nearby?"

He pointed across the road to a small motel. "Small but clean. Ask my wife for towels."

"How convenient." I did appreciate not having to call a taxi or Uber to get to a motel but wondered if the motel was built before the repair garage or later as a convenience for customers.

He smiled. "I'll call for the part now." He left me standing by the desk and went through the door into the repair area.

With nothing more for me to do at the garage, I walked across the road to the motel, pulling my small suitcase behind me. I found the mechanic's wife friendly and the room clean and smelling fresh, just as I had been told. A small card on the bed suggested the restaurant next door.

But first things first. I called Gunner and told him my story.

"Well, I'm glad we can get the repair done, but I won't have my favorite suit now."

That seemed like an odd remark. "You wouldn't have it if I was gone on another case. Just go to the men's store and buy one. Is that so hard?"

"But I wanted my favorite one." He sounded oddly whiny, like a three year old. "And I don't want to leave Mom and Kim to drive over and get it from you. Besides, I'm waiting for a call from New York. There's been some change in my travel arrangements for the tour."

I debated about telling him my idea to move to Willow Birch but changed my mind. I didn't get what was so important about the charcoal suit anyway. Considering his attitude, I told him to have a good trip.

I spent the rest of the day watching cable TV and sleeping pretty well. I was used to sleeping in hotel beds. The next day the mechanic showed me the damaged hose and gave me an itemized bill. I appreciated his fast service. "Tell your wife the room was nice—very comfortable," I said, giving him a quick wave goodbye.

7

I PULLED INTO THE DRIVEWAY AT SYLVIA'S HOUSE EARLY afternoon. I hurried into the house and found Kim on the couch and Sylvia sitting in the chair with her eyes closed.

Kim awkwardly pulled herself up to a sitting position. "Is Dad always so uptight when he leaves on a trip?"

"I can't say, honey. These last few years, I've been gone, so I don't see him packing or getting everything together. This time he wasn't able to open his closet and pick out the clothes he wants."

"I hope he calms down now that he's gone. He even had Gram nervous." Kim nodded toward Sylvia. "She's resting now."

"No, I'm not." Sylvia sat up straighter. "Gunner is just like his father. Albert always got so excited when he had to change something in his regular routine. 'Bout drove me crazy."

"So, what did you do when he was gone?" Kim leaned back.

A sly smile crossed her face. "Anything I wanted. I read a lot. Had lunch with friends and, of course, went to the fabric stores."

Kim's face shined. "Let's do that now. The three of us."

"Fabric? You need more fabric?" I thought they might want to go to a movie or to a play at a local theater.

"Fabric is my downfall," Sylvia said. "Always has been. Albert never understood that."

"Then fabric it is, Gram. I'll finish the alterations for Nancy Green this afternoon. We deserve a break for a day." Kim went to the dress form to change a section of a jacket.

Sylvia reached out a hand. "Sit and tell me about your trip."

There wasn't much to tell, especially since I didn't want to talk about selling the condo. The Christmas ornaments I'd brought back were supposed to be a surprise. Gunner and I needed to talk about George and a move before I mentioned it to either Sylvia or Kim. But all of that was on my mind. While the three of us were out, I saw two empty storefronts on Main Street that would be perfect for a lawyer's office, or maybe I could take over and use David McClure's old office. My mind was never at rest about George's suggestion.

———

While Gunner was gone, I spent more time with Sylvia and Kim, who could slow down a little now with Halloween behind us. We took three trips into Green Bay. Kim had a doctor's appointment there, and Sylvia found some yarn to knit an afghan for the baby. I found her working on it every evening. We stopped in a bookstore on one of our trips, and Kim found a book on caring for a baby for the first year. Another one to add to her collection. I had to smile when I saw Gunner's book in the window. A large photo of him sat next to the book with a sign reading *Local Author*. I took a photo and sent it to him and then called him, but my call went to voice mail. Just then, I wanted to hear his voice and tell him I loved him.

One evening I researched the steps I'd need to become a

licensed lawyer in Wisconsin. George had made it sound easy, and he'd been right. With some online courses and sample exams to study, I wouldn't have to leave Willow Birch except to take the state bar exam.

By the second week of Gunner's trip, Sylvia had rested enough from Halloween that she was ready to teach Kim and me her secret recipe for homemade noodles. "Every year, the week before Thanksgiving, Willow Birch has a Baskets of Bounty auction," Sylvia said. "This year, there are going to be fifteen baskets, so we need to make fifteen bags of noodles and some for ourselves."

I wasn't aware Willow Birch had so many events to help people in need in the small community. "So, what happens to the baskets?"

"There is an auction, and the highest bidder gets to choose a name on the list."

"And who would have the list?" I had the Anderson family in mind.

"George. Who else would know who needs help but is too proud to ask?"

I shrugged. "Well, you."

Her sly smile told me I had guessed right.

The night before the noodle day, Kim set out the eggs to warm overnight. I hefted the large bag of flour onto the counter, and Sylvia showed us how the noodles would dry on the antique clothes-drying rack. "I can remember my grandmother and mom using this same rack to dry their noodles." Sylvia seemed to be lost in a memory for a few minutes.

"I remember us making noodles when I came for visits, Gram."

"And remember how good they taste? So much better than the ones from the grocery store," Sylvia said, leaving that memory behind her now.

The next morning Sylvia had bowls and measuring cups and spoons ready. As if teaching children, she showed us each step of the measuring and mixing process. When Sylvia had Kim and me rolling the dough, she kept shaking her head that the dough wasn't thin enough. "Keep rolling, from the center to the edge. Lift the rolling pin, so you don't flatten the edges."

It was much easier to watch her roll a sample than follow her directions. Both Kim and I knew this was a skill developed over many years of practice, but neither of us would quit.

By afternoon the drying rack was full of hanging noodles. Kim was so tired she almost fell asleep at supper, but Sylvia had found a second wind and clapped her hands when she looked at our accomplishment. "When the noodles are dry in a day or two, we'll bag them and use fabric strips to tie the bags closed. Gram and Mom did that, too."

I told both of them to go on to their rooms, and I'd clean up the kitchen. There seemed to be flour everywhere, so I planned to mop the floor when I'd finished filling the dishwasher and hand washing the large bowls. Gunner called before I started. I could feel his excitement, though when I tried to talk, he didn't seem to listen. But when he said, "You need to come with me next time," I stopped trying to tell him what had been going on at home. Until that conversation, Gunner had never suggested that I be part of his writing world, maybe because our worlds were so far apart.

"I would like that, Gunner. I promise to be available."

My words stopped him. "Don't promise what you have no intention of fulfilling, Charlotte."

That threw me. I wasn't expecting to be challenged, especially not when we had begun to feel easy with each other again. "We need to talk when you get back to Willow Birch."

"About?" I heard hesitation in his voice.

"Our future together," I said softly.

"Do I need to worry?"

"Oops, no, no, nothing like that," I whispered, "but I have a few ideas that you might like."

Gunner sighed. "Only two more towns to go, and I'm

getting tired of saying the same thing over and over. How are Kim and Mom?"

His steamrolling seemed to be slowing down. I made light of our trips to Green Bay and our noodle day.

"I remember Mom making tons of noodles for the Thanksgiving baskets."

"I remember when we made them years ago, and your mom reminded us about all the flour that ended up on the floor." I stopped to see if he would add a memory. When he didn't, I said, "I really want to go to the auction. I hope the Anderson family is on the list of recipients. I can't forget the look in Alex's eyes or the condition of his clothes."

"You've seen a lot of bad people," Gunner said, "and other ordinary people like us in all kinds of trouble these last few years. Maybe it is time for a break."

"More for us to talk about when you get home," I said, still keeping my voice low. "Keep well, Gunner. We'll be waiting."

"I'm waiting to see you."

8

GUNNER'S MOODS HAD BEEN UP AND DOWN SINCE I'D COME TO Willow Birch. He'd been cold at first, only warming up when it was clear I was staying, at least for a while. Knowing Gunner and our history, he was likely waiting for me to leave for another case that would give me the challenge I said I craved. And boost my ego, which is what his book tours did for him. Since he left for his tour, I'd come to enjoy the more relaxing days with Sylvia and Kim. The longer we were together, the more fun we had. What an odd threesome we made.

The evening before Gunner's return, I was alone in the sewing room, enjoying some quiet time in front of the fire. Sylvia came into the room so quietly it was her movement that alerted me of her presence. "Charlotte? Is everything okay? You've been quiet today." She sat in the chair next to the couch.

"I'm fine. Just organizing my thoughts."

"Are you leaving?" She adjusted her robe.

"No. I don't think so. Not now. I'll stay to the end of the year like I promised Gunner. My life if different now since being here with you and Kim."

"I hope you find it better."

It would have been easy to say yes, but that wasn't necessarily true. "I don't know about better, just different."

"George Pearson called me this morning. He told me he suggested you stay in Willow Birch and open your own office."

My back stiffened. "Why would he call you?"

"He's serious about having a good lawyer for the people in the community. He knows that losing David McClure left many of us without an attorney we can trust." She shrugged. "I guess he simply wanted me to know that he'd approached you."

No pressure or anything. "Oh, please, people around here don't know me."

Sylvia shrugged. "We can change that quickly enough."

If Sylvia was suggesting an introductory get-together, I wasn't in favor of that approach. "What do you have in mind? I know from experience that being introduced to someone doesn't make you trust them."

"True, but if we announce that Kim and I have formed a partnership for a sewing business and you did the paperwork and filed the documents, maybe that would start the conversation, as they say."

"Whoa. You and Kim are forming a business?"

She put her finger to her lips. "Not a word about this to her. Do you understand? I haven't said yes...yet."

"But...but, her job?"

"She's never wanted to do anything but sew, but she wanted to make you happy, so she went to school to be a teacher. You put a high value on a college education. She knew you always thought my sewing wasn't a professional career."

"Is there enough work for you both to make a living?" I held up my hand. "Sorry. Forget I asked. It's none of my business."

"I don't need the money from sewing, but if you need assurance, ask Barbara for my financials."

"Barbara? My sister?" What more didn't I know about this family?

"She's been doing my taxes for years."

"That's also none of my business. Barbara and I don't talk about our clients. But let's get back to George here." I explained that I wasn't licensed in Wisconsin.

"George says it's..." She waved her hand.

"Only a matter of taking the bar exam." I smiled. "I know, I know. George pointed that out to me."

Sylvia wrapped her robe tighter around her body. "When George gets an idea, he'll move mountains to see it accomplished. I remember when he thought Willow Birch needed a community center, and he badgered the town council until they agreed with him."

"Like someone else I know." I gave her a smile. "But some days, Sylvia, I feel like I've lost control of my life." My honesty surprised me. Besides, George was being awfully presumptuous.

Sylvia laced her fingers and rested her hands on her chest. "I don't think you've had control for a long time, Charlotte. But what I think of control surely isn't how you define it."

Puzzling. But we were talking in circles. Two generations of women who saw life differently. The third generation suddenly popped into my head. "So, if Kim partners with you, where will she live?"

Sylvia frowned as if I'd asked a question with an obvious answer. "I suspect here with me and the baby. Why do you ask?"

"Well, I asked because I was wondering if she can afford an apartment, plus childcare."

"Are you offering to take care of the baby?"

I couldn't believe that was a serious question. "Me? Even if I wanted to and didn't have my career, I don't think it would be fair to the baby."

Sylvia waved me off. "You keep minimizing what you can do. You've taken care of all of us since you arrived."

I gave her a pointed look, but maybe she was right. I had found a degree of satisfaction helping my family, and maybe opening a practice in town would be enough of a challenge.

Sylvia stood and put her hand on my shoulder and gave a light squeeze. "I would love for you and Gunner to live here with Kim and me." Then she patted my shoulder a few times before leaving the room.

Live with Sylvia and Kim? And a baby?

Like one big happy family? Four generations of it.

I felt a jolt of energy travel through me. I wished Gunner was here so we could consider Sylvia's offer.

———

WE TURNED GUNNER'S HOMECOMING INTO A CELEBRATION. I made lasagna and a salad for supper. The smell of garlic filled the kitchen from the meat sauce and the steaming bread. We sat around the table a long time and grilled Gunner about the cities and towns he saw on his tour and the people he met. By the time we were done, Gunner had put together a day-by-day travelogue. Perhaps sensing Gunner and I wanted to be alone, Kim and Sylvia left for their rooms when we'd polished off dessert.

I began to clean up the kitchen while Gunner enjoyed another cup of coffee, but before I finished, I sat down and took one of his hands in mine. "I'm very glad you had a successful tour, Gunner. We missed you—I missed you."

He leaned forward and gave me the kind of kiss I longed for. "Been a long day. Let's get the kitchen ready for morning and head upstairs."

Our routine for morning was automatic now, so it didn't take us long before we were going up the stairs. He fell asleep quickly, so I tucked the comforter around his shoulders and kissed his forehead. There would be time for us to talk in the days ahead.

My plans for a long discussion with Gunner never materialized. Sylvia's friends and neighbors stopped by to visit her, but they really wanted to talk to Gunner. He was between books and was enjoying more relaxed days. I heard him laugh more and tease Kim about making him a grandfather. He never let her forget it. Some days he was happy with that thought; others he moaned about the passing of time and his age.

———

STRONG WINDS HOWLED THE EVENING OF THE BASKETS OF Bounty auction, bringing falling temperatures and a threat of snow flurries. At the last minute, Kim decided to stay home. She was being extra careful not to get chilled and end up with a cold. Sylvia offered to stay with her, but Kim knew this event was important to Sylvia and refused her offer. She promised her grandma to call if she needed help.

With no time to waste, Sylvia, Gunner, and I loaded the back of Gunner's SUV with bags of noodles and hurried to the Community Center. Sylvia introduced me to the event coordinators when we arrived, and we were greeted by other residents who'd filled huge boxes with homegrown vegetables and kitchen ready foods. We added the bags of noodles to each box.

The coverings over the windows from the Halloween event had been removed, but the lighted trees in the corners added a glow to the room. Each table had a centerpiece fashioned from straw. I saw scarecrows, cornucopias, and baskets of Indian corn.

We found a table where Sylvia could sit and participate. She'd told me how sad she was that so many families needed help other than food. I saw it as part of her pitch for Gunner and me to relocate to Willow Birch. I had a feeling Sylvia saw me doing a lot of cases *pro bono*.

I was the first to bid when the auction began. I was determined to get a box for the Anderson family. That wasn't guaranteed since there were more families on the list than boxes to give out. I was lucky, though, and my bid was the highest. The basket would be delivered the next day to the Anderson home.

When the evening ended, I found myself thinking about George. I wish he'd been able to see the community's generosity for himself.

————

THE NEXT WEEK SYLVIA MADE LISTS TO KEEP US ORGANIZED FOR Thanksgiving. As she'd done for years, Barbara was due to arrive on Wednesday afternoon. Our table would be full when Sylvia invited Lester and John. Sylvia ran the Thanksgiving show and appointed me to keep track of the grocery list. She liked to start the holiday with a big breakfast, and the next item on her agenda was watching the Macy's parade on TV. Gunner made hot chocolate as a treat to have while they watched the parade, another tradition.

Gunner held up his coffee mug. "I can scare up some hot chocolate this year if you'd like." He pointed to me. "Add that to the grocery list."

Sylvia had the schedule figured out down to when we'd start setting the table, which was also when we'd get the rest of the meal ready. "By the time we start that stage, the turkey should be about three-quarters done. Oh, I wish we had a bigger table." Sylvia would have invited many more people to her table if she had the room.

When I finally had a chance for a serious sit-down talk with Gunner, I had a long list of Sylvia's wishes to talk about. My own list was growing right along with my growing excitement to upend my life and move to Willow Birch.

9

LESTER AND JOHN KNOCKED ON THE DOOR ON THANKSGIVING Day as Santa Claus and his reindeer ended the parade. Lester brought his customary jar of honey, and John had a bouquet of cut flowers. He'd fashioned what I was sure was a one-of-a-kind wooden carrier for the glass vase.

The banter led to a wager on one of the afternoon football games. I didn't know much about football, but Barbara sure did. She surprised us all when she ticked off the names of the offensive and defensive players on her favorite national team.

Gunner tried to pass off the job of carving the turkey, but we all ganged up on him and more or less demanded that he do the honors. We filled our plates with dressing and sweet potatoes and cranberries. Sylvia had made her traditional apple-cranberry pie and a from-scratch pumpkin pie. Lester's favorite, as it turned out.

Any one of the family favorites on our table could compete with all the five-star restaurants I'd ever been to. "We'll need to make sure the traditions will live on with our new generation coming along," I said, smiling at Kim.

"Good idea." Kim looked down and patted her round belly. "Bet you'd love to taste Gram's pumpkin pie."

"Hey, everybody," Barbara said, tapping her fork on her water glass. "Before we all scatter, I have an announcement to make." Barbara smiled at John. "I'm going to start my own accounting and tax business here in town. I'm launching in January."

Kim and Sylvia said simultaneous "wows." I was too surprised to respond.

"Actually, it's two businesses," Barbara said. "I also want to develop my decorating crafts into a shop called *Especially For You*."

Kim clapped, and John put his arm around Barbara's shoulders. Sylvia had tears in her eyes. Gunner grinned. I sat dumbfounded. "Why? How? When? Tell us more."

It wasn't so complicated once Barbara explained her decision. She loved to sew, and with Kim having a baby, Sylvia would need more help. She reached across the table to take my hand. "I love the sewing, and being with the whole family reminded me how lonely I've been lately."

"And I'll need all the help I can get with the baby," Kim pointed out.

Barbara drew her hand back from mine and put it over John's. Well, well. Another family member keeping secrets. Even Kim had yet to tell us if she was having a boy or a girl. Or, maybe she decided she wanted to be surprised herself.

Always the practical one, I asked, "Have you rented a place?"

She nodded to John. "We're going to look at one of the vacant buildings on Main Street tomorrow. John can tell me if it is a good investment. The listing says there's an apartment upstairs."

Sylvia waved her arm to get Barbara's attention. "I told you, there's no need for you to rush to find a place. There is plenty of room in this big house for all of us."

Barbara grinned. "I appreciate that, but I want to get situated as soon as possible, so I can be ready for business come the first of the year."

Now, I really wanted to talk to Gunner. If he agreed, it wouldn't take us long to move to Willow Birch, and our family would all be together. Barbara and I could end up working on Main Street in a matter of weeks.

I got to my feet and started to organize the cleanup with Barbara helping. I shooed Sylvia, Kim, and Gunner out of the room to go watch football with Lester and John. My ulterior motive was my desire to be alone with Barbara to find out more about her plans.

Barbara stopped stacking plates and leaned against the counter. "The decision was easy. I like Willow Birch. I love working with Sylvia, and I don't find any joy living alone and being so far away from family."

"You were always welcome to visit us in Minneapolis anytime. It's not that far from Superior."

Barbara rolled her eyes. "Oh, sure. When would that have been? In the last two or three years, you were gone more than you were home."

"What about leaving your friends?" I handed her a large glass platter.

She shrugged. "Most of them have families or work a second job."

"So, you're not doing this on impulse." It was more of a statement than a question. I wanted to ask her about John and if she saw their relationship becoming more than friendship. Maybe it was too soon for her to know.

"Exactly."

Lester went home while we finished cleaning the kitchen. Time was ticking down on the game, with Gunner and John's team winning by a lopsided score. They didn't mind leaving the game to take off for a late afternoon walk. The air was crisp, but not cold, and a light breeze scattered the fallen leaves. Most of the tree branches were already bare.

Gunner and I walked behind Barbara and John. I hadn't seen my sister so animated in many years. I didn't know what they were talking about it, but it must have been funny because their laughter echoed in the air and filled my heart. Barbara had needed time to grieve our parents' death, and for over a year while still a senior in high school, it seemed she'd lost direction for her life. When I showed her what we were paying the attorneys to probate the wills, Barbara decided on an accounting and tax career and did it with laser focus.

With Barbara and John walking arm in arm, Gunner and I might have disappeared, and they wouldn't have noticed. Barbara waved to Lester, who was standing in the window when we passed the Grant home.

"These older homes are so beautiful, aren't they, Gunner?" I remarked. "When I was in Minneapolis, it struck me that our condo seems so sterile and modern that we'd never say it has character—or personality."

Gunner nodded. "Hard to believe a building can have such a lonely feeling to it." Gunner waved to Lester.

"We're going to visit with Lester for a while, you guys. You're welcome to join us." Barbara was careful with her words, but I noticed she didn't reach out to encourage us to come inside.

"Sure, we'll join..." Gunner started.

"You go ahead," I said, talking over him. "Gunner and I haven't had much time together." Barbara and John went up the steps and into the house.

"Why did you do that?" Gunner asked.

"Because it was obvious Barbara wanted to be with John, and she needs to get to know Lester a little. They don't need us hanging around."

Gunner stopped walking. "Are you doing a little match-making here?"

I groaned. "Like I had anything to do with it. Barbara and John found each other all on their own." I reached down to pick up a bright red maple leaf that had perfect edges. I twirled it between my fingers, making it look like a pinwheel.

I held on to the leaf when we returned to a quiet house. Kim was resting, apparently after declaring she ate too much. Sylvia was working on the baby's afghan by the fire and encouraged us to join her. "Two holidays done and one to go. I think we should get the tree on Sunday. Don't you agree, Gunner?"

"So soon? We're not finished with Thanksgiving yet. Tomorrow we'll have turkey and dressing sandwiches." He patted his stomach. "But if that's what you want, Mom, we'll do it."

"I trust you and Charlotte, and Barbara, if she'd like to come along, to pick the best tree for our small corner."

When Sylvia had converted her living room to a sewing room, most of the furniture had been shoved to the edges of the room or was stored upstairs. As I looked around the room, I saw that if we moved the sewing machines closer together, we could fit in at least one more chair. Sylvia and Kim didn't have that much sewing work left before the holiday. "If we move..."

Sylvia nodded, but Gunner said no.

"But why? We don't have enough room for us all to sit together without dragging one of the sewing chairs over."

Gunner shook his head—and with some energy. "No, and no, again. We move furniture every year, and last year, we moved furniture and tables and brought chairs down from upstairs. For four people. Four," he emphasized. Apparently, Kim sat on the floor near the tree, which left plenty of room for Gunner and Sylvia on the couch. Barbara sat on the chair Sylvia was using.

I had no rebuttal. I'd promised to be in Willow Birch for Christmas, but a huge winter storm buried the Midwest and I spent Christmas at the O'Hare Airport.

In a wry voice, Sylvia reminded us again to get a small tree, or none of us would be sitting near it. She also reminded us about the Christmas decorations in the attic. "Shouldn't we take advantage of this mild weather to hang the outdoor lights and garland?" she suggested, with a note of humor.

I suppressed a loud snicker. Sylvia was a master at getting people to do what she wanted. She didn't issue orders to people to do her bidding. She didn't need to. She just brought them around to her point of view. What a talent. One I wanted to develop.

The attic was located above the garage, with access through a door in the room Gunner used as an office. When we stepped in, I was astonished by the number of boxes and trunks lining the walls. Most boxes were labeled with Sylvia's handwriting. Five generations of Wilsons had homesteaded the land and built the house that began a legacy.

Gunner piled the same boxes of garland and lights they'd used last year near the door, and we took a couple of trips to move them into the living room to deal with tomorrow.

Kim joined us by the fireplace about the time Barbara came back. She looked so pretty with her face just slightly flushed. I couldn't believe the enormity of the gift my sister had been given in meeting John Grant. She looked happy, and her life was changing fast.

"You want to join us when go out to get a tree on Sunday?" I asked.

Barbara fidgeted with her dangly earring. "Um...well... John and I were going to get one for Lester. But why don't we all go together?"

"Count me out," Kim joked. "I'm not going out anymore unless it's to the hospital. "I scooted down the couch and crowded Gunner so Kim could bring her feet up onto the cushions. I patted her ankles, which were swollen more than they were a few days ago. It struck me Kim never complained about things like her ankles or her backaches and never talked about how dramatically her life had changed.

When we closed out the day, I rushed my nightly walk through the house checking on doors, and now that the nights were colder, the thermostat for the furnace. All was well.

I rushed upstairs to talk to Gunner before he drifted off into a sound sleep. Gunner was lucky that way. He could sleep anywhere, and he'd perfected the art of the power nap. I sat on the edge of the bed and took his hand. "Hey, Gunner," I whispered, "I want us to go away together for a couple of days."

He immediately removed his hand from mine. "No. Not now..."

"Wait, hear me out. I'm just talking about a couple of nights in Door County. We need to do some Christmas shopping and buy a few things for the baby. Barbara is here now, and if Sylvia or Kim needs anything, she can handle it. And we'll be less than two hours away."

He still was doubtful, but he'd stopped shaking his head. He let out a light laugh. "You and me. *Alone* for two nights?"

"You catch on fast," I teased. "Yes, alone. But before you go down that shiny road, we also need to talk about our future. More mine than yours, but our decisions will affect our whole family."

"So talk."

I shook my head. "When I start, I don't want to be interrupted."

"Spoilsport."

I bent forward to give him a kiss. "Sleep well, my husband. I'll make reservations before you change your mind." Gunner was fast asleep by the time I got off my laptop. I crawled in bed next to him and smiled. My plan was coming together.

10

WITH FOUR OF US AT THE TABLE FOR BREAKFAST, I KEPT AN EYE on the doorway for Kim. The tea and coffee were done about the time she plopped into her chair. "Sorry, I fell back to sleep."

"No problem," I said. "We aren't rushing today. Or sewing. But I don't think we want to take on Black Friday crowds." That brought unanimous agreement.

"Well, if that's the case, I need helpers outside to hang the lights and the garland." Gunner flashed a self-satisfied smile.

"Aren't you smug?" I teased. "You caught us off guard."

"Then I'll make the most of it while it lasts," he teased back. "We'll plan to get the tree on Sunday, like you asked, Mom." He gave her a nod. "Then I'll have fulfilled my holiday obligation. I'll leave the rest of it to all of you."

I passed around the dish of toast, made from fresh home-made bread, a gift from one of Sylvia's friends, made even more delicious with Sylvia's raspberry jam. "I have news, everyone. Gunner and I are going on a shopping trip to Door County next week, Tuesday to Thursday."

Sylvia stirred her tea, although she'd already added her

honey, so she was only keeping her hands busy. "Wonderful idea, Charlotte. Gunner isn't writing at the moment, and he needs to get away."

Gunner almost spit out a mouthful of coffee. "I just got home. I was gone for two weeks."

"So? That was work. This is for fun," Sylvia countered. She switched the banter to the topic of sewing. Only two outfits remained on the dress form and mannequin. Final fittings were scheduled for next week. She and Kim were in good shape in terms of work. Sylvia was keeping her promises to her clients.

As we cleaned up the kitchen, Barbara mentioned she had no plans to go back to Superior just yet.

"I assumed that. We wouldn't have planned the trip if you weren't going to be here," I said. "We can't leave either of them alone now." I gave my sister a quick one-arm hug. After our parents died, we'd relied on each other, but that closeness had lessened over the years. I wanted to be those sister-pals again.

On Sunday, just as Gunner had predicted, the tree lot was filled with families running from tree to tree in their quest to choose the perfect one. John had come along, and he and Barbara took one path through the tree farm, and Gunner and I took another. No one wanted to show up with a tree that didn't exactly match Sylvia's requests. With more than one hundred trees on the lot, it was a daunting job to find the perfect tree, especially since I found something wrong with each tree I looked at.

Finally, in frustration, Gunner took one off the rack and paid the attendant before I could object. "Mom will love this one. Looks like the one we had last year, you know, tall and green."

I playfully swatted his arm before grabbing the top of the tree to help carry it to John's truck. We found Barbara and John enjoying hot cider inside the large building loaded with wreaths and loose boughs. Barbara insisted on buying wreaths for Sylvia's and Lester's front doors.

I rubbed my hands together. "Boy, it's chilly in the wind." I pulled my hat off and finger combed my hair.

Gunner wrapped a lock of my hair around his finger. "I like it longer."

I reached up to smooth fly-away strands. I hadn't even thought about my hair since I'd cancelled my hair appointment in Chicago. That was over a month ago. It used to be my haircut was critical to my courtroom persona, but I could relax about that now. I doubted anyone in Willow Birch cared a thing about my hair.

At home, Gunner and John set our tree in the stand and wiggled it into the small area Sylvia had pointed out.

I stood behind the couch. "See, if we'd moved..."

Gunner drilled me with his look of impatience. He shook his head no.

I held up my hands in surrender. "Okay, you're right. It's fine where it is." Why did I care, anyway? It was only a tree, and it would be out of the house in six weeks or less.

The next day we ferried boxes of decorations and ornaments down from the attic and placed them on the floor near Sylvia. Our decorating became a Wilson family history lesson when Sylvia told us a story about each handmade ornament, some dating back to her grandmother's day. We'd heard the stories before, but it was fun to hear them again. We hung the ornaments Gunner made in school in the front.

When most of the boxes were empty and Barbara was cleaning up the clutter, I ran upstairs to get the boxes of ornaments I'd brought from Minneapolis. When I returned, I handed one box to Kim, who was trying to get comfortable on the couch. "Maybe you can find a spot for a few of these."

She stared at the box while I sat next to her.

"Just open the box," I said, "you'll see."

She unwrapped the first ornament and gently fingered the

wings of the delicate angel. The tag read "Baby's First Christmas." "Oh, Mom, I forgot about this one." She laid it aside to unpack the rest in the box. I sent a quick text to Gunner to ask him to join us downstairs.

When he came into the living room, Kim handed him a couple of ornaments. "Here, Dad. You put them on the tree like we did when I was little."

Right then, I made a promise to myself that I would never miss another Christmas with my family. The room became silent as each of us was lost in private memories. I remembered the years Gunner and I were together with Kim and made the road trip to Sylvia's an adventure. I also remembered being alone when I hadn't made it back to Minnesota from a case and spent the holiday in a hotel—or an airport, like last year.

I handed a second box to Barbara. "These have been packed away for too many years." Her memory was much better than mine. She remembered every one of the old ornaments that had been part of our childhood.

"Thanks, Charlotte. I thought these had been thrown away years ago."

"I did, too, but then they turned up." Unlike Kim's, Barbara's angel had a broken wing. She didn't seem to mind.

That evening we sat around the tree with its lights aglow and a warm fire. We were making our lists of gift ideas for us to exchange or for Santa to bring. Of course, Kim had the longest list. She claimed it was because half of the list was for the baby.

We had a good laugh when Barbara asked for paint and new flooring. Then she invited us to see her new house that next day.

———

As it turned out, the building was perfect for two

businesses. The big street-side windows would be perfect for her to showcase her crafts. One of the rooms down the hall would be her tax office, and there was a roomy two bedroom apartment upstairs. After checking the apartment, Gunner went downstairs to join Sylvia and Kim, but Barbara touched my arm to keep me with her. "This is all happening so quickly," she confided. "It's a little scary, but I'm too excited to let the scary part hold me back."

"And John?"

A giggle escaped. "That's scary too, but I'm going to go for the gold, sister. Just like you did with Gunner. Wish me luck."

I gave her a hug. "I do, I do."

———

ON THE DRIVE TO DOOR COUNTY, GUNNER ASKED IF I'D GIVE him a clue about what I wanted to talk about. "Authors give their readers all kinds of clues before the climax at the end of the story."

I gave him an "oh, please" look before I laughed.

It was early evening when we checked into our hotel, and we ordered room service for supper rather than going out. Gunner looked over the wine list and finally settled on a bottle of burgundy. As soon as our meals and wine were delivered and the door clicked closed, Gunner opened the bottle and filled our wine glasses. "Enough postponing, Charlotte. What's up?"

I started with George's suggestion and surprised him when I mentioned Sylvia and Kim were forming a sewing partnership, which meant Kim would be staying in Willow Birch.

I had more to say, but I ended the first part by saying, "I want to live in Willow Birch. According to George, I can easily switch gears and open a general practice. The town needs a lawyer for everyday things. I can be that person."

Gunner stayed silent, but he swished the wine around in the glass as he let what I said sink in.

"We could use the money from the sale of the condo to put an addition on Sylvia's house. The kitchen needs an upgrade, and we could have a large family room big enough for all of us. I want a fireplace in that room."

I could see from his gaze he was listening, so I kept going. "And opposite the family room, we would add rooms for us, sort of like a mother-in-law wing, only it would be for us."

"My, my." Gunner smiled and put a stuffed mushroom in my mouth. "You have been a busy girl."

I didn't think he was making fun of my ideas, but I'd caught him off-guard.

"And..." I started in again.

"There's more?" His eyes twinkled.

"Oh, lots more." I played into his mood.

"Okay, then," Gunner said, "here's a different take on your house plans." Gunner thought Kim and the baby, who wouldn't always be a baby, could stay downstairs, if Kim wanted to share this kind of four-generation living arrangement, at least for a while. She wouldn't have to deal with stairs, and we could have the entire upstairs to ourselves. "Nice, huh?" he joked, wiggling his eyebrows.

"Absolutely," I said, wiggling mine back.

"So, you're willing to give up your current work and open a practice in Willow Birch?"

"That's the plan," I said. "George seemed a little heavy handed at times, you know, kind of pushy. But when I thought it over, it's not a bad idea."

"Just be sure, Charlotte," Gunner warned. "It sounds good, but it's a big change for you."

I nodded. "It is, but it's what I want. More than that, I think *I* need it."

"Okay, then, as long as you're sure. I can do my work anywhere." Gunner smiled and then abruptly changed the direction of our conversation to the subject of Christmas and baby shopping.

I rubbed my hands together. "I plan to melt my credit card. I hope the car is big enough for everything I plan to buy."

"Onward," Gunner held up his glass of wine.

11

————

GUNNER AND I HAD A DISAGREEMENT ON OUR FIRST STOP. I wanted to snap up a wooden cradle, but Gunner felt strongly about asking John to build a cradle if I wanted one. "John's just come back to Willow Birch, and there's not much construction work in the winter. Better to hire him."

"You're right. I'll call him when we get home, but no spoiling the surprise."

That led to a discussion of asking John to build the addition onto Sylvia's house. I thought it was a terrific idea.

Suddenly, Gunner started laughing. "You know, maybe we should ask Mom if she really wants us living with her. I mean, Kim has moved in. Now we're talking about making this permanent and even building a new wing onto *her* house. We could just buy our own house."

"I thought she told you she'd love having us live there?" It was kind of funny, though. I'd more or less made a lot of plans based on the assumption Sylvia would agree to them.

"I've had that feeling for a long time." Gunner was serious now. "Every time I leave, she gets real quiet, and you should have heard the panic in her voice when she called to tell me she had pneumonia."

"True. Even with all her friends nearby, she's still alone when we leave." I met his gaze. We'd ask Sylvia, but we'd likely answered the crucial question.

The next morning, Gunner made a pot of coffee in our room using my favorite beans he'd brought from home. "Ah, you remembered to bring my favorite," I said, happily taking the cup from his hand.

"I aim to please." He saluted me with his cup brimming to the top with steaming coffee.

"Then let's check out and shop our way home," I said eagerly. "I can't wait to tell Sylvia and Barbara and Kim that we're selling our condo, and we're staying in Willow Birch. It's not every day we make big decisions like that." I reached over to take his hand. "We have a lot to do before I start a new law practice and you hibernate to write your next book."

As we packed up to leave, Gunner asked me about using my last case as a framework for his new book.

"Oh, great. 'Lawyer suffers a setback when client is found guilty after promising the client's family he'd go free?' How thrilling...for me."

"No, no." Gunner waved his hands. "Not anything that autobiographical. I was thinking along the lines of the young man's life after being found guilty and the reality of going to prison. Or, how his family's money can't buy his way out of prison." He shrugged. "I'm not sure."

"As long as no one can identify my clients or the case for real, I suppose it's okay."

I could see it coming. Gunner had idea after idea for his book, and that put him in his own private world. It didn't matter if we stopped to browse through an interesting shop or when we loaded the car with packages, Gunner's mind was on his writing.

By the time we finished lunch, I was done shopping and suggested we head home. No more than two miles down the road, my phone buzzed.

"Don't answer that. This is our time to be alone," Gunner tapped the steering wheel.

"Wishful thinking, Gunner. Kim or Sylvia might need us." I took the phone out of my purse and glanced at the screen.

"Pull over. Now!" I yelled.

I'd gotten his attention, and he immediately pulled onto the shoulder of the road.

Barbara had sent a picture. I turned my phone, so he could see what was on the screen.

A baby.

I called Barbara and, in my rush, dropped the phone. I scrambled to retrieve it. "Barbara?" I put my phone on speaker mode.

"Calm down, Charlotte. Everything's fine. Kim and the baby are fine. She named him Christopher Gunner Wilson. How about that?" Barbara laughed. "She's resting now, and so is Sylvia. It's been quite a night."

"Are you sure they're both okay?" I wanted to hear everything.

Barbara laughed again. "She named him Christopher because he was born so close to Christmas."

Gunner grabbed the phone. "Where are you? We're on our way home."

"We're all at the hospital, including Sylvia. I'll call if we leave."

"No, don't leave. It won't take us long to get there." Gunner disconnected the call.

I turned to him. "Hi, Grandpa." I couldn't relax the smile on my face. "But I have to wonder why they didn't call us when she went into labor?"

"Maybe the labor went fast. I guess we'll find out soon enough." Gunner checked the mirrors and merged onto the highway. "I can't believe it. I'm a Granddad."

"And he has your name, Gunner. You can be so proud."

Gunner parked in the visitor lot, and we followed the signs

to the maternity wing. At the desk, I took a breath. "Our daughter, Kim Wilson..."

The nurse pointed down the hall. "Popular new mom. Last room on your right."

The door was open, so we stepped in. Sylvia was resting in the lounger covered by a blanket. Barbara and John were on one side of the bed, talking softly. Kim had her eyes closed, so I guessed she was sleeping.

"Even John's here."

Gunner nodded, but my voice had roused Kim. "Hi, Mom, Dad. Sorry we cut your getaway short, but Christopher wanted to be part of our family sooner than we'd planned."

"How are you, honey?" Gunner stepped to the bed and kissed his daughter on the forehead. "This is a beautiful surprise."

"We're good, better now that you're home. You make us feel safe." She grabbed his hand.

I lightly pushed Gunner to the side. "You look wonderful, Kim." I looked around the room. "Where's the baby?"

"He'll be back soon. He's in the nursery. They'll bring him to me again soon. I want to hold him all the time." She smiled and lifted her shoulders in a happy shrug.

The sound of a crying baby got louder, and I turned to the door as a nurse was pushing a bassinet into the room. She more or less ignored us and waited while we got out of the way.

"He certainly knows when he's not near his mother," the nurse, smiling at Kim. She lifted Christopher and nestled him in Kim's arms. "Call if you need help, but by the way it looks you'll have all the help you need." She smiled and nodded as she left.

I stepped forward and peered into Christopher's face. His blue hat with the white pompom had moved down his forehead, so I gave it a gentle push up. He opened his eyes and scrunched up his face. "Now, that's not the way to meet your grandma for the first time."

I pulled the chair John had vacated closer to the edge of the bed and sat down. Kim touched my hand. "Do you want to hold him?"

"Of course." Kim and I hadn't dealt with the issues that had kept us from being close, and she hadn't filled us in about what happened with her boyfriend, but we had time to talk about all of that in the future. My eyes misted. "Yes, Kim, I'd love to hold him. I promise to give him back when he fusses."

I heard Gunner and Barbara chuckle.

I gathered Christopher into my arms and held him close. When he wiggled, I held his head and put him in front of me so I could see his whole face. "Christopher, this is your Grandma Charlotte talking, so listen up. I give you my Christmas promise that I will always love you." He held my finger tight like he would hold me to that promise.

Yes, it would be a wonderful Christmas at the Wilson house.

EPILOGUE

Four months later

THE SOUND OF CONSTRUCTION HAMMERING AND THE CLANKING of cement trucks had cleared Sylvia's house of people. Kim had taken Christopher to Barbara's office where she had helped Barbara get *Especially For You* opened in record time. Gunner had offered to rent a room at Lester's house so he could write, but Lester refused any money. "We'll be family soon from the looks of it." Barbara and John had been inseparable since Christmas. Sylvia was now out with friends after a winter of being housebound. She'd liked to stay nearby in case Kim needed help with her great-grandson. She hadn't stopped smiling since Christopher arrived.

I sat upstairs in Gunner's writing room, working my way through sample exams posted online for the Wisconsin bar exam. I would be traveling to Madison that next week to take the test. I had put off taking the bar exam in January and February to move our things from Minneapolis to Willow Birch. It took Gunner and me more than a week to pack our personal belongings and arrange for a mover. By that time, January had bled into February. Gunner had made himself scarce during the day to begin writing his next book. Sylvia was pleased that calls for tailoring requests for spring and Easter outfits were more frequent now.

One weekend we helped Barbara move into her newly painted apartment. With John and Gunner doing the heavy lifting, we women unpacked the numerous boxes of household items and craft supplies. I missed having my sister in the house with us, so some mornings I went to her place for a visit before she opened the shop.

My phone buzzed, taking me out of my practice exam and my thoughts about the changes in my life. I was surprised to see George's name on the screen. I got up to close the door and muffle some of the noise.

It seemed George had been doing some thinking, too, and before I knew it, he proposed a partnership. "You know, you and I together can do some good in Willow Birch and make a living, too. I've been thinking..."

He was off and running, and twenty minutes later, George and I had agreed to a partnership and had hashed out a few details.

Before we said goodbye, I promised George I would tell Gunner the news.

"Oh, Charlotte," George started, "about promises..."

I laughed.

The End

Thank you for reading *The Christmas Promise.*
If you enjoyed this book, please tell a friend or leave a review
online to help other readers discover my books.
Thank you!

ABOUT THE AUTHOR

In a world of abundant books, Gini Athey always finds herself reading three or four at the same time. While she reads across genres, her favorite books involve families with all their challenges and rewards. She writes the stories she likes to read, those that involve families and their dilemmas.

For years ,Gini has found great joy in making quilts for family and friends. She has done many for weddings, baby gifts, and house warmings. She enjoys visiting quilt shops, knowing that being around fabric brings out her creative spirit.

Gini and her husband are avid world travelers and enjoy summers in their camp in Canada. They live in a rural area west of Green Bay.

Gini is the author of the heartwarming small town series, The Shops on Wolf Creek Square. She is currently working on a new series. For more information, visit her website at www.giniathey.com.

.

www.ingramcontent.com/pod-product-compliance
Lightning Source LLC
Chambersburg PA
CBHW022038170626
46808CB00003B/1261